angel P9-DDM-693

"The company is now depending on you."

The executive turned and faced Jan directly. "Kyle Masters will allow us to film the house and the Christmas celebrations there—on one condition."

"And that is?" The words came out in a hoarse whisper as Jan's hands clenched to white-knuckled tautness.

"That Capital Films do the filming, and that you're part of the team, my dear."

Jan's face paled. "You can tell Kyle Masters that I won't be made part of any deal!" she snapped, rising to her feet. Whirling in her mind like a series of kaleidoscopic impressions was the face of Kyle Masters: now tender, laughing, loving; now harsh, punishing, hating. The changeable face of the man who had been her husband...still was her husband....

Return to Silvercreek

by

ELIZABETH GRAHAM

Harlequin Books

TORONTO • LONDON • NEW YORK • AMSTERDAM
SYDNEY • HAMBURG • PARIS

Original hardcover edition published in 1978
by Mills & Boon Limited

ISBN 0-373-02237-9

Harlequin edition published February 1979

CHAPTER ONE

JANICE BROWN sighed as she handed over her section of the month-end report to a bespectacled girl clerk. Capital Films had exceeded their own record for non-production for the month of October, and Jan knew that no company, least of all one devoted to capturing offbeat subjects on film, could subsist only on the occasional contract which had come its way recently. Inflation costs, combined with the unalterable fact that more and more television and documentary outlets were doing their own filming, had made assignments more difficult to come by.

Not that Capital didn't have the best in cameramen and documentary writers. Bernie Stover and Hank Linden couldn't be bettered at capturing and encapsulating the salient points of a story on film, while John French brought to life in words the rock-bottom despair of Vancouver's derelicts or the vivid art world of the West Coast with equal facility. Nor could Don McLeish, the owner and driving force of Capital Films, be faulted for his untiring efforts to make his company the best and most reliable in the business.

Jan sighed again when a vision of Don's athletic, fair-haired figure came to mind. Dynamic, fast-moving, fast-talking Don who could very easily have become an important factor in her life over the past two years. The holding back had been on her part entirely. She knew that a man like Don McLeish deserved better than that. He should have someone who was breathlessly, ecstatically in love with him to share his life ... not a woman who had loved that way once and never would again.

She started when the phone at her right hand rang,

5

and her voice was faintly husky with emotion when she answered it.

'Jan?'

Don's voice held the sharpness of concern, and Jan cleared her throat to say: 'Yes, Don, it's me. Did you want me?'

There was a barely perceptible pause, then Don spoke in the guarded tone which indicated that some outsider, possibly a badly needed client, was in his office with him. 'Can you spare a few minutes to come along, Jan? There's someone I'd like you to meet.'

'I'll be right there.'

Pausing only to check that no strands of her glossy black hair had escaped from the chignon at her nape, and to brush pale lipstick on her well-defined mouth, she hurried along to Don's office. Capital's office layout was far from extensive, yet Jan was sure she had formed half a hundred prayers on her way to Don's more spacious room only a few steps from her own small domain. Fervent hopes that the man she was to meet was about to offer them an assignment. It was as she raised her hand to tap at Don's frosted glass door that a frown settled faintly between her dark brows. It wasn't usual for Don to consult her before committing himself to a project—why was this occasion different?

Traces of the frown lingered when she entered the adequately sized room and saw a tall man, his hair iron grey, rise from a chair beside the desk to join Don, who stood behind it. A look unfamiliar to Jan flitted across Don's face before he averted his eyes and said heartily:

'Sorry to drag you away, Jan, I know you're busy, but Mr Godson here wanted to meet you. He's representing the Timberline Lumber Company, which might want us to produce a film for them.'

'That's wonderful.' Ignoring Don's blatant untruth as to how busy she was, Jan took a step forward and found her hand clasped between bony fingers. 'I don't believe we've done any work for your company before,

Mr Godson, but I'm sure you won't be disappointed in our standards.'

Cool grey eyes warmed slightly in a smile. 'Such loyalty to the company is unusual these days, Miss Brown.'

'Mrs,' Jan corrected briefly, and took the chair opposite the lumber man's. 'When you get to know us better, you'll realise that loyalty and genuine enthusiasm are usual throughout Capital Films. We take pride in knowing that our work is the best available in Western Canada at least.'

'You've a very clever saleslady—*Mrs* Brown,' Frank Godson turned to say drily to Don. 'It seems a sinful waste to hide her away in one of your back offices.'

'Janice is hardly hidden away, Mr Godson,' Don protested with a laugh that sounded forced to Jan. The violet of her eyes met the lighter blue of his with a puzzled cast. 'She's my right hand—left too, on occasion.' His eyes sobered to seriousness without shifting from hers as he said quietly: 'I don't know what I'd do without her.'

'Neither, I'm sure, would Mr Brown,' the older man said, only a faint suggestion of a twinkle in his eyes as they went over Jan's dark hair and perfectly oval face, retroussé nose which imparted an air of femininity to her profile, and mouth hinting of warmth and laughter though her lips at present were pressed into business-like lines.

'There's no Mr Brown,' she replied coolly, forestalling further enquiry in that direction by staring levelly into Frank Godson's eyes until his dropped.

His murmured apology was lost in Don's jovial: 'Mr Brown's loss is definitely my gain, Mr Godson! Now,' he shot Jan another look, 'maybe you'd like to explain to Jan the set-up for your film.'

'Certainly.' The lumber man cleared his throat and turned his body in the chair until he faced Jan directly. 'We're anxious to do a film on our areas of operation— lately there's been a lot of controversy with people who think we're destroying the environment of the Interior country with our logging operations there.' He seemed to notice Jan's stiffening as he spoke and his brows rose in enquiry. 'Are you one of the conservationists, Mrs Brown?'

'No-no,' Jan admitted, her mouth dry suddenly. 'I've no objection if there's selectivity in cutting. There's nothing so desolate as mountain after mountain stripped to black-stumped baldness.'

To her surprise, Frank Godson chuckled. 'I agree with you. But even if Timberline wanted to create such devastation—which we don't!—our present largest supplier wouldn't have it. He has thousands of acres of virgin timber, but you'd think every tree meant something special to him.'

'It probably does,' Jan said faintly. 'I—I know a little about the country and the people there, and——'

'So I understand,' Godson put in smoothly, surprising her again. 'We want to show the public on film that we're not the ogres some people say we are, but a film devoted entirely to clips of selectively cleared hillsides would be a little boring. So we thought it would round out the picture if we interspersed scenes of an ordinary family enjoying Christmas in the Cariboo. As it happens, our main supplier owns the most picturesque and historic house in the area, and he'll allow us to film the house and the Christmas celebrations there—on one condition.'

'And that is?' The words came out in a dry croak as Jan's hands clenched to white-knuckled tautness.

'That Capital Films do the filming, and that you're part of the team, my dear.' Obviously expecting her to be gratified, Frank Godson seemed shaken by her white-faced fury.

'You can tell Kyle Masters that I won't be made part of any deal!' she snapped, rising agitatedly to her feet and pacing away from Godson's shocked expression.

'You obviously know our supplier, Mrs Brown,' he blinked. 'But——'

'Yes, I know him,' she returned bitterly. 'Too well to let him——'

'Leave it to me, Mr Godson,' Don inserted smoothly, rising to his feet so purposefully that the other man followed suit, though his eyes still lingered bewilderedly on Jan's averted back.

'Fine, fine,' he said nervously, picking up his briefcase from where it leaned against the desk. 'Let me know as soon as possible if the deal's on.'

'I'll do that.'

Jan scarcely heard the older man's departure, or Don's return to the room a few minutes later. Whirling in her mind like a series of kaleidoscopic impressions was the face of Kyle Masters—now tender, laughing, loving ... then harsh, punishing, hating. The changeable face of the man who had been her husband ... still was her husband ...

'Jan.' Don closed the door and crossed to her, halting abruptly when she rounded on him in blind fury.

'Just what do you think you're doing, Don? You knew I'd never agree to a scheme like that!'

He held up a placating hand, then went thoughtfully to sit on the outer edge of the dark polished desk. Folding his arms across his chest, he said quietly: 'Don't you think it's about time you faced the facts, Jan? You can't run away from Kyle all your life. Sooner or later the question of a divorce has to be settled. You know that.'

'If that's his idea in blackmailing me to go down there he can think again! There's such a thing as a postal service, even in the back of beyond.' She paced restlessly again, frowning and biting a thumb nail nervously. 'How did he know where to find me? I'm not listed in the phone book, and finding a Brown in a city this size is like looking for a needle in a——' She broke off abruptly and swung back to look anxiously at Don. 'Do—do you think he knows about Robbie? He couldn't, could he?'

Don shrugged. 'It seems he knows quite a lot about

you, and about Capital. He always seemed a determined type to me.'

'Oh, he's that all right—but he's ruthless too, once he's set his mind on doing something.' Her brow cleared. 'That's why I'm fairly sure he doesn't know about Robbie—if he had found out, he'd have turned Vancouver upside down looking for him, not caring if he trampled me in the process!' She went to put a hand on his arm. 'Don, I'm sorry, I just can't do what Mr Godson asks. I can't take the risk of Kyle finding out he has a son. He'd find some way of taking him from me.'

Don's capable hands came down to rest heavily on her shoulders as he looked directly into her tension-filled eyes. 'Now that's just plain stupid thinking, Jan, and that's not like you. Nobody can take Robbie from you.'

In spite of his reassurance, Jan shivered. 'You don't know Kyle as I do, Don. He'd find some way to get and keep his own son, and I—oh, Don, I just couldn't bear to be parted from my baby! He's my only reason for living.'

The brief spasm of pain that crossed Don's face was missed by her because her head was buried in the comforting breadth of his shoulder, her voice muffled with tears.

'You won't lose him, honey,' he murmured, tightening his arms round her slender frame for a moment before holding her away and dabbing at the smudged mascara beneath her eyes with his handkerchief. 'Look, it's almost time to quit for the day anyway, so why don't we go find a nice quiet spot to have a drink and talk things over?'

'I can't, Don,' she sniffed. 'But thanks. Robbie——'

'Robbie's not going to come to any harm if Hilda has to take care of him for an extra half hour. She hasn't poisoned him yet, has she?'

'No,' she admitted, smiling. 'It's just that I see so

little of him, I hate to give up any of my precious time with him.'

But Don was adamant, and fifteen minutes later they were seated in a secluded alcove in the dimly lit bar not far from the office. The two or three other customers were seated at the bar chatting to each other and to the bartender, so Jan and Don had all the privacy they wanted for their talk. But Don waited until the waiter had brought the Martini he had ordered for Jan and the light beer for himself before he spoke.

'Look, Jan, I'm not being completely altruistic when I urge you to go through with this Cariboo Christmas thing. You know the state of our finances—this could see us through for a month or two anyway until things pick up again. There's a good possibility we'll get the South African job to do then, but without this one now we may have to fold long before spring when the action starts.'

'Oh no, Don!' Jan stared at him aghast. Capital was the wellspring of life to the entire team, and it was impossible to think of it, and the vital energy Don had poured into it for six years, quietly disappearing overnight.

Don gave her a whimsically dry smile. 'Oh yes!' He sobered. 'But I want you to believe me when I say that there's no way on earth I'd ask you to go there if I thought it would bring harm to you or to Robbie. Do you believe that, Jan?'

'Of course I do,' she breathed, her eyes misting as she laid one fine boned hand over the bigness of his. 'I owe you so much, Don ... so very much. Without your help, I——'

'You owe me nothing,' he said roughly, turning his palm up to meet hers and bringing his other hand down to cover them. He kept his eyes lowered there while he went on quietly: 'You've been very special to me ever since the day you came into Capital looking for a job ... eighteen and eyes full of wonder like a young doe's.

I wanted to pick you up and carry you off to my cave right then, but you were so young ... it wouldn't have been fair. Then hardly a year had gone by when you met Kyle Masters, who swept you away and married you before I had time to draw breath and tell you how I felt.'

'Don, I'm so sorry,' she whispered. 'I really didn't know—then. Maybe if I had——'

He shook his head and sat back, releasing her hand. 'It wouldn't have made any difference. Nobody else existed for either of you once you'd met each other. That's why I couldn't believe it when I found you wandering around Vancouver looking for somewhere to settle long enough to——'

'To have my baby,' she finished for him softly, memory of his goodness making her eyes shine with a luminous glow. It had been Don who had taken her to his own apartment when dozens of hard-eyed landladies, perceiving her condition, had blandly told her their vacant room had been taken. No one had wanted to bother with a young soon-to-be mother who wore a slim gold ring on her marriage finger, their steely downward glance disbelieving its genuineness. No one had wanted to offer her shelter—no one but Don, who had demanded nothing more of her than that she make herself comfortable in his apartment to await her child's birth. It had been Don who had taken her to the hospital and waited the long hours until Robbie made his appearance, Don who had festooned the apartment with flowers for their return from the hospital. Don who had been deeply hurt when she had insisted on leaving to make a separate life for herself and her child. She had, however, permitted him to give her back the job she had filled before her marriage, her determination strong to prove her gratitude in that way.

'You never did tell me exactly what happened between you and Kyle,' Don now interrupted her thoughts, holding up a hand when she frowned and shook her head. 'I've never pressed you for details, knowing it was none of my damn business—though I couldn't begin to put a number to the nights I lay sleepless planning what I'd do to him if I ever met up with him again.' His voice was grim, supplementing the steely look in his eyes. 'But I'd like to hear a little more now, Jan, so that I know just what you're facing if you go back there.'

Jan looked away into the gloom just beyond their table, her eyes distressed as remembrance tumbled through her mind. Like a camera clicking in never-ending sequence, she saw in turn the old rambling house made of weathered logs, the huge inner hall which also served as living room, the high panelled dining room leading from it on one side, Kyle's office opposite. Next to that, and just before the curving sweep of stairs to the upper galleried hall, was the small sitting room Kyle had told her would be hers when his grandmother no longer needed it.

Her mind balked at envisioning the stairs that led to the room associated with the greatest happiness and deepest despair she had ever known. The bedroom she had shared with Kyle.

'Jan?' Don coaxed gently, and she brought her bemused gaze back to the fair-skinned face with its anxious expression. Harsh memories coloured her voice.

'There isn't a lot to know, Don. We'd been married six months when Paul Steel, Kyle's friend from university days, came to spend Christmas with us. He and Kyle could almost have been brothers as far as looks went—dark hair, eyes, the same lean build except that Kyle was a few inches taller. But in personality they were completely different. I doubt if Paul ever thought beyond the next moment in time, whereas Kyle——' She hesitated, taking a deep breath before going on in a voice that seemed half buried in painful memories. 'Kyle thought everything out very carefully before committing himself to a course of action ... I think even he was surprised when he proposed to me after knowing me for only a few weeks.' The dark blue of her eyes echoed the bitterness in her voice as she went on: 'So that what happened—or what Kyle *thought* happened—later was something he'd half expected.'

Don leaned slightly towards her. 'He thought you and this Paul had fallen for each other?'

She nodded, sadness etching the outer area of dullness in her remembering eyes. 'Yes. Paul had always been able to take away any girl Kyle was interested in at university ... we'd been laughing about it over the Christmas holiday, and I thought Paul was joking when he told Kyle, one night after he'd been drinking more than usual, that he could take me away from him just as easily. Kyle didn't say anything, just smiled in that quiet way of his ... afterwards, I realised Paul looked on that smile as a challenge.'

'So he went all out to prove his point?' Don frowned disbelievingly.

Jan nodded again. 'Not that it mattered, I thought. Kyle knew I loved him; he was everything to me.' She gave a twisted smile. 'When you've been brought up in an orphanage and foster-homes, not knowing whether your surname really is Brown, or Smith, or whatever, it's really something to be loved by a man who not only shares his life but his name with you. Anyway ...' she frowned and bit her lip.

'Don't tell me any more,' Don interjected, his voice grown husky.

She shrugged. 'You might as well hear the rest of it. Kyle was called away unexpectedly for a few days ... it gets very cold up there, you know,' she added with seeming irrelevance. 'Cows were dying because their water holes had frozen over, and Kyle had to take a few of his men and break holes in the ice.'

A shudder ran over her as remembrance clouded her eyes and she went on tonelessly: 'Paul hadn't touched me all the time Kyle was away—I'd even enjoyed his company, because Kyle's grandmother never left her room—but the night Kyle came back, Paul came into the bedroom. He'd heard Kyle drive up to the house, and thought it would be a joke for him to come into the bedroom and find us together.'

Don swore softly. 'But Kyle didn't regard it as a joke?'

'No,' Jan smiled mirthlessly. 'What man would, coming into his bedroom and finding his wife in a wispy nightdress being kissed by his best friend? I— I was trying to push Paul away, but to Kyle it looked as if I was ... was ...'

'But surely he knew you better than that?' Don burst out. 'My God, you'd been married for six months! Just because of a friend playing the kind of practical joke he was used to, Masters couldn't have believed——'

'You don't understand, Don,' Jan interrupted tersely. 'None of the girls Paul took from Kyle had been important to him—his wife was a different matter. Deep down, he thought he'd been too impulsive in marrying me, I guess, and what he saw convinced him he'd been foolish. And to a man like Kyle Masters, being considered a fool—even by himself—is more than his pride can take.'

'So he threw you out.'

Jan hesitated fractionally. 'Yes. Paul and I left first thing in the morning.' Not even to Don could she confide the horror of that last night at Silvercreek House, the cold, passionless taking of her body by the husband whose former tenderness mixed with fire had brought her to the upper peaks of a love she had never thought to know. A night which had resulted in the conception of their son ... a child born of punishing hatred ... the boy Kyle had wanted to carry on the Masters name at Silvercreek ...

'Wh-what?' she asked, bewilderment crowding her voice when Don interrupted her thoughts.

'I said,' he repeated patiently, 'there's no need for Kyle to know that Robbie is his son. As far as he knows, it's just as likely that Paul Steel is the father.'

Jan winced, her eyes glancing off the mild blue of

his. 'He'd know. Kyle has the mind of a steel spring trap; he'd work out the time span in two seconds flat.'

Don rubbed his chin thoughtfully, looking at her. 'Not if you told him the boy's birthday was in October rather than September.'

She stared at him uncomprehendingly for a further moment, then made a dismissing gesture with her hand. 'He'd still know, Don. Robbie has his dark hair, eyes, skin—he couldn't be mistaken once he saw Robbie.'

'But you said Kyle and Paul were similar in colouring—couldn't Robbie be Paul's son just as easily as Kyle's?' Don's soft voice insinuated itself into her subconscious mind and worked there unobtrusively. The thought had never occurred to her before, but of course it was true. Robbie's dark hair and eyes could equally well come from Kyle or Paul. Only her own biased discernment could see the same hesitant tilt of dark brows before a smile of devastating sweetness lifted the full curved mouth of both her son and her husband; the frown of concentration on Robbie's immature brow when he played with an intricate toy mimicking the more deeply etched lines on his father's face. Even to the slight but noticeable inward and downward curve of his chubby small toe on each foot, Robbie was his father's son.

'It would never work, Don,' she said with desperate certainty, knowing that however much Don and Capital Films needed her, she could never take the risk of Kyle discovering the child was his. So strong had been his desire for a son that she knew instinctively he would do anything to keep Robbie once he was aware of his existence.

'Why wouldn't it?' Don persisted, eyeing her narrowly. 'There's no reason for Kyle to know he even has a son—it's you he's asked for at Silvercreek at Christmas. He doesn't have to see Robbie at all.'

'But—Christmas!' Jan ejaculated, horror darkening the violet of her eyes. 'I couldn't possibly leave Robbie with strangers at Christmas!'

Don's brows lifted quizzically. 'Strangers?' he asked. 'You can hardly class Hilda and Johann as strangers!'

'But——' Jan's voice trailed off disconsolately as she realised unwillingly that Robbie was far more used to Hilda and her boisterous young family than to herself. However much she disliked the idea, she was simply the one who came home in time to give Robbie his bath and supper and tuck him into bed. The bigger part of his waking day was taken up with the Svensen family and the noisy excitement they generated in his two-year-old mind. If she were to be absolutely honest, she knew that Robbie would be far happier sharing the Christmas holidays with the Svensens than in solitary state with a mother who adored him.

'Look, there's no need for you to work yourself up into a state about something that might never happen,' Don said with a crispness unusual for him away from business. 'Masters wants you—the team—down there within two weeks, and nothing will be settled until then. If he gives you the go-ahead, there's no reason why we couldn't shoot the entire film then—a mock Christmas dinner shouldn't be too hard to set up. You'll be back here in good time to spend the holiday with Robbie.'

'And if Kyle doesn't agree?' Jan asked quietly.

Don shrugged. 'Then we'll call the whole thing off. Who knows, something else might turn up before we have to make that decision.'

CHAPTER TWO

But no other assignments came Capital's way, and ten days later Jan, her bags packed, hugged the small body of her son to her and buried her face in the dark sheen of his thick hair. To his small mind, this parting was no different from the ones that took place every morning, and he pulled resentfully away from the too-tight hold of his mother's arms and looked at her with darkly puzzled round eyes.

'Do not worry,' Hilda said gently from beside them. 'I will take care of him like one of my own, you know that.'

Jan managed a watery smile before kissing Robbie's plumply rounded cheek one last time. 'I know, Hilda,' she choked, thrusting the strong young body to the fair-haired woman's waiting arms. 'I'll phone as often as I can, and—I should be back within a week.'

Not looking back, she sped blindly from the pleasant old-world house and took her place beside Don in the mobile film truck. The other men would follow them to the Interior in the large motor home they used for accommodation when filming at out-of-the-way places. On the occasions when Jan accompanied the team as production assistant, a curtained-off area at the rear of the motor home provided separation and privacy for sleeping. Apart from Don, the men were married and with another kind of woman there might have been a few family arguments about these arrangements, but Jan was well liked by the wives. This was partly due to an unspoken assumption that Jan and Don were a twosome, but mostly because they trusted Jan not to overstep the friendship she shared with them. Besides, they knew that their husbands would eat a more balanced diet when Jan was there.

Don tactfully ignored the tears she tried to wipe surreptitiously from her eyes as he concentrated on driving out of the city towards the mountains visible on the far horizon. Jan watched with sightless eyes as the ribbon of freeway was swallowed by the powerful vehicle, the ache in her heart increasing with every mile.

But why should she feel this parting from Robbie more acutely than any of the others? Was it because his father lay at the end of this journey, the man who must never know his son existed? Was this sinking, hurtful feeling an upsurge of guilt because she was hiding from Kyle the knowledge that could make him a happy man? But was it wrong for her to do so, knowing that Kyle's happiness would spell the beginning of her own misery?

Misery was a familiar companion of Jan's. Abandoned by the mother who had given her birth a few days previously, she had spent most of her young life in institutions or in foster-homes which were sometimes loving, sometimes callous. Although the anonymous surname of Brown had been given to her, her Christian name was her only legacy from an errant mother. Such a small clue in the riddle of her identity, but Jan had long since given up the futile efforts of imagination which spun webs of fantasy around parents who were young and madly in love but unable to marry.

Such a background had given Jan an underlying lack of confidence in her own worth as a person, in her ability to give and receive love. That was why, when Kyle Masters came into her life, she had found it difficult, if not impossible, to believe that such a man found her desirable enough to want to spend the rest of his life with her.

Strong, handsome, forceful, master of untold acres of wild and beautiful Cariboo country, the great-grandson of pioneers in that part of Canada's vast wilderness area—Kyle was all of these things, the ideal man of many women's dreams. But those qualities in him had not been all of her reasons for falling deliriously, deeply and completely in love with him. In fact, they had played a far lesser part than the gentleness she discovered in him, the deep soft core at the heart of him, the side he hid from the world he moved in—a world where men were strong and women independently sturdy. Women like his grandmother, who had brought him up in her own autocratic ways after the death of his parents when he was a child too young to know the enormity of his loss.

Jan sighed and glanced out at the rapidly passing fields where sleek cows cropped the mudstained tufts of grass in the Fraser Valley. It was old Esmeralda Masters who had stamped her own stiffnecked principles on the grandson she possessed with the greedy fingers of age. A woman who deeply resented the young bride Kyle had chosen, because of her inexperience in the ways of ranch life and because Janice Brown the foundling was not the wife she herself had selected for Kyle when he was still a boy ...

Another sigh escaped Jan at the immediate inner vision of Elena Pearson, only child of a neighbouring rancher, whose fair good looks and knowledge of ranching made her a far better prospect as a wife for Kyle than her own city-bred self. Elena had, with scarcely veiled insolence, made it clear at their every encounter that Jan was the one big mistake in Kyle's life. How happy she must have been when she discovered that Kyle had dismissed Jan from his life as if there had never been love between them ... no nights of passion and underlying tenderness in the big bedroom they shared on the upper floor of that historic house; no sudden desires as they lay on the narrow strip of sand bordering the lake behind the house after a moonlight swim ... desires that demanded fulfilment from the store of love between them ...

Don's hand suddenly covered hers on her lap and

squeezed it. 'Just play it as it comes, honey,' he said gruffly. 'Don't ever forget that I'm there if you need me.'

Jan found it difficult to speak past the lump in her throat. 'Thanks, Don,' she managed, and felt a swell of thankfulness for his solid strength which would never let her down. Don would never have believed, as Kyle had, that another man could come even remotely near to stealing the affections she had given him in the fullness of love ... that she could dream of lying in another man's arms after knowing the bliss of being possessed by the one who filled every fibre of her being with joy, needing, wanting.

That part of her had been dead for more than two years now. Long gone were the nights when she would wake with tears on her cheeks, tears induced by dreams of being held in strong sinewy arms that made a mockery of her lonely childhood. A voice echoed from her dream the words Kyle had whispered on their wedding night. 'Now you'll never feel alone again, darling. For a while you'll just have me, and then when our children come along, you'll have the family you've never had.'

Her lips twisted in bitterness. How glibly the words had been spoken, how easily forgotten! Hate was akin to love, it was said, and the measure of her hatred for Kyle now could only be fathomed by the depth of the love she had borne him once.

Perhaps now was the time, as Don had suggested, to cut the tenuous ties she still held to Kyle. Divorce, and a fresh start—with Don? Don loved her, had loved her for years ... and she was fond of him. Robbie even called him 'Daddy' in imitation of Hilda's children who welcomed their father home every day with boisterous enthusiasm. Would it be so wrong for her to share the life Don had offered on more than one occasion? Maybe in time his kisses would inspire the same spark of desire, the longing for oneness with another human being, that Kyle's had. Wouldn't she forget, given enough time, the hard warm strength of Kyle's mouth on hers, the work-roughened hands, long and well shaped, that held magic in their ability to caress her body and make her forget everything but her need to love and be loved?

The film crew joined them halfway through lunch at a prearranged spot. As if sensing her super-sensitive state, they kept up a spate of lightly bantering conversation throughout the meal. They all knew, of course, that Kyle Masters was her husband. Jan had met Kyle on one of their filming forays, and all of them had been loud in their disapproval of her marriage to 'Mr Superman', as they jokingly called Kyle. To their credit, not one of them had made any comment on her sudden reappearance as an employee of Capital Films or the fact of Robbie's existence. Whether this was due to Don's explanations and request for strict privacy as far as Jan was concerned she had never known, but she had appreciated their seeming lack of curiosity.

As they rose to continue their journey Hank, whose lugubrious expression hid a deep vein of humour, said: 'Mary's put together an interesting meal for us tonight—at least, she's thrown in all the ingredients for a spicy Mexican dinner we had on our vacation down there last month, and I guess she's trusting to the gods that you'll know what to do with it, Jan.'

'I'll think of something,' she promised, 'even if it's just boiling it all up together.'

They emerged into the pale November sunshine with varying expressions of distaste on their faces for the unappetising sound of the meal awaiting them later, then John French, as immaculately dressed as ever in what he called his 'backwoods' clothing of cashmere jacket, whipcord slacks and camel waistcoat, said:

'Maybe our host will take pity on us and provide a reasonable meal. My digestive processes rebel at the thought of food seasoned to Mexican tastes in this cool zone of ours.'

Jan glanced at his craggily shaped face under carefully brushed brown hair and saw colour rush under his skin in an unusual display of embarrassment.

'I wouldn't count on an invitation if I were you, John,' she said quietly.

'I'm sorry, Jan. I—forgot for the moment that he's not only our host, he's——'

'My husband,' she supplied, her eyes going round the small group of men. 'I'd be grateful if you—if all of you—would have the same kind of forgetfulness while we're at Silvercreek. As far as I'm concerned, this is just another job, even though I expect to clear up some personal business while I'm here.'

Don's head swivelled round, his eyes meeting and holding hers in unanswerable question. Then, while the other men made consenting murmurs of 'Sure, Jan' and 'If that's the way you want it, Jan,' he wrenched open the passenger door of the truck and gestured for Jan to get in.

'The forgetfulness covers Robbie, too,' he said harshly. 'He doesn't belong to Masters, but he could make a lot of trouble for Jan trying to prove the child is his.'

Jan sat silently beside Don's broad figure as they swung out again to the highway and headed north. Finally, she said in a small voice: 'I—I hate lying to them. Was it absolutely necessary?'

'Absolutely.' Don glanced across at her and added drily: 'They're all fathers, Jan, and their loyalties could lean more towards Kyle than you if they knew you were hiding his son's existence from him.'

She subsided into silence again, watching the rolling hills slide past the side window, her thoughts in turmoil as they had been since knowing of this trip back to her past ... the past she had thought dead and buried. Kyle had made it only too clear, that last night at Silvercreek House, that he never wanted to see her again. Why, then, this sudden demand for her presence? Was it that he had grown tired of the married yet unmarried state? That he wanted to marry again? Elena, presumably, if that was the case. In defence against the stab of pain this thought gave her, Jan turned to Don's frowning profile as he watched the road ahead.

'I meant what I said back there, Don,' she said, her voice more highly pitched than usual. 'I'm going to settle things with Kyle once and for all ... agree to a divorce if that's what he wants.'

Don's brows lifted slightly, though his eyes remained on the front. 'As you pointed out yourself, Jan, if he'd wanted only that he could have taken the necessary steps without forcing you to come down here.'

'You don't know him,' she told him bitterly. 'He can be kind and generous and—and loving, but there's another side to his nature that would let him relish flaunting another woman before me. The fact that I haven't taken steps towards a divorce might have made him think I still care...'

'And do you?' Don queried enigmatically, still not looking at her.

Her head turned sharply round to stare at him incredulously. 'What's that supposed to mean? How could I still care for a man who professed undying love for his wife, but wouldn't believe her innocence when that love was tried?'

'I don't know,' he shrugged. 'Women are strange creatures—they usually tend to stay in love with the first man who stirs their senses.'

'Then I'm the exception to the rule,' she snapped, sitting stiffbacked in her seat and gazing angrily through the windscreen. 'I've told you, I mean what I say. I'm going to tell Kyle that I want out, and—if you still want me when he's out of my life for good, then ...'

'Don't commit yourself to something you might regret, Jan,' he put in, his voice hard yet conveying the knowledge that he could be hurt if for some reason she couldn't keep her word. 'I've waited this long, another few weeks won't be too hard to take.'

Jan gasped. 'A few weeks?' she echoed. 'A few days—a few hours!—are all I need to set Kyle Masters straight, however many prospective brides he parades before me!'

She spoke vehemently, but Don's glance in her direction held a thoughtful look. 'We'll see,' was all he said, and an uneasy silence fell between them until they had forked left some fifty or so miles south of Williams Lake and were surrounded by Masters land on either side of the gravelled road. Cows recently brought down from summer pastures further north, sleekly well-fed from the succulent cropping there, thickly dotted the pastures. Kyle was a top-rate rancher, Jan admitted grudgingly, noting the mended fences running for miles along the roadside. During her short marriage she had learned that good men were hard to come by and that much of the work was done by Kyle himself. Three years ago, the basic number of seven permanent employees was augmented from time to time by itinerant cowhands who would stay for a while before moving restlessly on to other pastures.

Her heartbeat grew quicker as they approached the homestead area, then slowed to a dull numbness when the house itself came into view. The only thought in her deadened mind was the hope that this numbness would last and see her through the initial meeting with Kyle. However deep the channels of hatred ran in her, she was honest enough to admit that nurturing hatred was a far easier thing to do from a distance.

Suddenly she sat up with a jerk, her eyes widening in astonishment as the house came closer. It was the same structure she had known so well, but with startling differences which made her breath draw in sharply. It looked now like the hazily dreamed plans she and Kyle had made during the long winter evenings spent before a blazing log fire in the living room ... evenings when they had sketched plans for renovation of the exterior and interior without taking away the authenticity of the historic layout ... plans executed between kisses that more often than not had led to the sketchbook being pushed aside and forgotten ...

Now lawns stretched in vague outline in front of the house, immature shrubs sheltered by the leafless branches of stolid shade trees hugging their perimeter yet leaving room for the beds of annual flowers Jan had pictured blazing there.

The house itself had the soft gleam of new varnish covering the staunchly contoured logs, shutters painted in pale lemon to match the pillared rail fence enclosing the wide veranda. The scarred wood of the old front door had been replaced by the satin sheen of cedar, the thickness of which could be gauged even at this distance.

Jan's heart tumbled, her mind spinning dizzily as Don drove a few hundred yards to the more open spaces between neatly painted red and white ranch buildings. Kyle had followed the plans they had made so faithfully ... was it possible this meant that he still cared? Was this his way of showing her, Jan, how wrong he had been, that he regretted——?

All such thoughts died as she leapt from the vehicle and saw two figures emerge from one of the barns. Elena's bright blonde hair was easily distinguishable beside the crisp dark brown of Kyle's. The tremor that invaded Jan's being at sight of Kyle's tall figure and easy stride gave way to coldness that frosted the deep blue of her eyes as the two drew closer. Was Elena already living here, sharing Kyle's work—and his love? But no, his grandmother would never agree to that kind of arrangement.

Nevertheless, the thought gave Jan the courage to face unflinchingly the cool appraisal of Kyle's dark eyes set deep over high cheekbones and clearly defined jaw, which had already grown darker by the progression of the day. Lines deeper than she remembered etched the sides of his mouth ... a mouth firmly held, but showing a tendency to generous fullness ... a mouth capable of raising her to the heights of a passion never dreamed of ...

'How are you, Kyle?' she asked coolly, then turned

her eyes to Elena's slightly flushed face. 'And you, Elena?'

'We're just fine,' the fair-haired girl said levelly, answering for both as she tucked a possessive hand through Kyle's bent arm. 'You look well.' Her pale blue eyes swept over the russet pants suit Jan was wearing, and suddenly Jan was glad that the suit she had chosen brought out the dark sheen of her hair and gave an added tone to her skin.

'You remember Don McLeish, Kyle?' she said as Don came round to stand beside her, so close that she could sense the staunch protection his well-knit body provided.

'Very well,' Kyle spoke for the first time, his eyes moving from Jan to take in Don's protective stance beside her. A faint sardonic smile edged his lips as he held out a hand to the other man.

Perhaps only Jan noticed the slight hesitation before Don put out his own hand to grip the rancher's briefly, but the smile deepened on Kyle's lips, revealing a glimpse of strong white teeth.

'Welcome to Silvercreek, McLeish—though I understood this preliminary visit was for Jan only.'

Jan looked sharply up at Don's impassive face and before she could stop herself, said: 'But I thought ...' Her voice dwindled into silence as she looked from Don's blank expression to the steely look in Kyle's eyes.

'You asked for Jan as part of a team, which she is.' Don's head swivelled round as the sound of the approaching motor home reached them. 'The rest of the team is arriving now.'

Kyle's eyes narrowed on the cream-coloured vehicle as it pulled up beyond the truck. 'The arrangement was that the entire team show up at Christmas time when—Jan and I have sorted out the details.' His eyes switched to Jan as he spoke, but moved quickly back to Don. Unnoticed by anyone but Jan was the loose falling away of Elena's hand from his arm.

'A film company works as a team, Mr Masters,' Don

replied evenly. 'You either have none or all of us.'

For the space of a second or two the men's eyes met, then Kyle shrugged nonchalantly. 'It's up to you whether you want your men to stand idly by while Jan and I come to terms.' His gaze flicked Jan's briefly before returning to Don. 'You can park over there by the barn. There's a tap for water, and the men's bunkhouse facilities can be used.'

'Thanks,' Don returned drily, then turned to glance appraisingly at Jan before joining the rest of the team. 'Coming, Jan?'

'In a few minutes, Don. You go ahead,' she said, then, seeing his hesitation, flashed him a reassuring smile. 'What Kyle and I have to talk about won't take long.'

She felt strangely bereft when his broad figure turned away, a feeling emphasised by the fact that Elena seemed not to have taken the hint that she wanted to talk to Kyle alone.

'If you'd like to come up to the house,' he said now, 'I can rustle up some coffee or whatever else you'd like to drink.'

'I'm sure the entire team would appreciate a hot drink at this point,' she returned tartly, but stepped out ahead of the other two, defying her steps to falter as they approached the house, so familiar yet so strange. At the top of the few steps leading to the front porch she paused, waiting for Kyle to come from behind her to throw open the thickly wooded door and usher the two women inside.

A gasp she couldn't suppress burst from Jan. As in a dream, she looked round the hall-living room which looked as if the old interior had been scooped out and a new one installed ... the one she and Kyle had envisioned so long ago. In place of the old-fashioned fireplace they had lain before in love was a breath-catching expanse of roughcast grey rock reaching far up the wall to the galleried bedroom floor above. An arched fireplace, capable of receiving logs of immense proportions, dominated the room and drew the eyes to a cosy arrangement of sofa and chairs placed to enhance the intimacy of the hearth area. Rugs of white sheepskin and black bearskin enhanced the soft patina of gleaming hardwood floor, and the broad staircase leading to the floor above was covered now with a dramatic sweep of flame-coloured carpeting.

Speechlessly she looked at Kyle, the question in her eyes dimming to mute appeal for explanation as they met the noncommittal brown of his. But Elena's high-pitched voice broke into a thousand fragments the fragile web of what might have been communication.

'What do you think of the changes, Jan?' she chattered, linking her arm with Kyle's again. 'We've had so many problems getting it just the way we wanted it, haven't we, Kyle?'

'There have been—problems,' he answered slowly, his eyes fixed on Jan's. 'Do you like the new look of Silvercreek House, Jan?'

Jan blinked as if waking from a dream and detached her gaze from his. 'It's—very impressive,' she answered, glad that her voice could sound so matter-of-fact. 'But what does your grandmother think of all the changes?'

'I've no idea,' he returned blandly. 'She died eighteen months ago.'

'Oh. I'm sorry.' Her perfunctory reaction to the news of Esmeralda's death simply echoed the dislike she had known for the matriarch during her lifetime. Without her vindictive interference in their lives, who knew what the state of their marriage would be at this moment? That Kyle had seen his grandmother before coming up to confront herself and Paul in their bedroom was obvious from the grim lines round his mouth when he opened the bedroom door. Had his grandmother filled his ears with false tales of passionate encounters during his absence? A sigh escaped Jan's lips. What did it matter now? The old woman was dead . . . as dead as the love that had once been between Kyle and her.

'I'll ask Hannah for some coffee,' he said now, pausing first to set a match to the laid fire and satisfying himself that the flames would catch and hold before disappearing with his long-legged stride to the rear of the house. Jan shivered as she took his place before the leaping flames and realised how cold she had been.

'I'd forgotten how cool it can be at this time of the year here,' she said without looking at Elena, who had followed her to the sitting area, shedding her pile-lined blue jacket as she came.

'It's really not that cold right now,' she returned, but her back nevertheless seemed to appreciate the growing warmth from the fire. 'Wait till the snow comes —but then you won't be here, will you?' she interrupted herself silkily.

'What makes you so sure of that?' Jan countered, glancing away from the leaping flames momentarily to watch the wind-whipped light complexion of the woman beside her. Her skin was flawless, although she was five years or more older than Jan.

'Kyle just wants to clear things up between you so that we—so that he can live the life he wants.'

'With you?' The stinging colour that flooded Elena's cheeks had nothing to do with the warmth from the fire, and Jan felt a cold sense of satisfaction in baiting this woman who had set her sights on Kyle years before he had met Jan. Like the crab, she would lose her claw before giving up voluntarily that which she coveted.

'Yes,' Elena returned unequivocally. 'I've been in love with Kyle for as long as I can remember. And now —after his disaster with you—he knows that no one else could be the wife to him that I could.' Her pale eyes had a slant of condescending pity in them as they slid over Jan. 'You really had no idea of what it was like to be a rancher's wife, had you?'

'Have you any idea of what it's like to be a *wife*?' Jan said caustically, rewarded by the deepening of Elena's rosy flush, though the other girl recovered her equilibrium almost immediately.

'That comes naturally, doesn't it?' she returned smoothly, 'whereas fitting into an alien background is something else again.'

Jan swallowed the biting comment that rose to her lips and instead looked round the room appraisingly. It was so different, yet achingly familiar in its new look ... a look that had been only a misty picture in her mind's eye three years before.

'What do you think of the changes we've made?' There was challenge in the question as she moved away from the fire to drop casually, familiarly, into one of the softly cushioned armchairs stationed at either end of the hearth.

'*You've* made?' Jan raised one delicately arched black brow, unable to stop the disbelieving words.

Elena laughed. 'You don't think a man as busy as Kyle has had time to supervise all this as well, do you? He had very definite ideas as to what he wanted, but he left it to me to see that the work was carried out.'

Oh yes, Jan thought bitterly, he had very definite ideas about the way he wanted the house to look! Ideas and plans he and she had formed together on this very spot. The stir of gripping fingers at the pit of her stomach made her switch her gaze from Elena to the leaping flames licking the dry logs to crackling warmth. What had made Kyle use, to the last detail, the plans he and the wife he now despised had dreamed up together? Nothing in his coolly appraising eyes at their meeting even remotely suggested that he still cared, that he realised how wrong he had been about Paul. No, she sighed inwardly, it was more likely that he had nurtured his unreasoning hatred all this time and had now brought her here to torment her with the obvious fact that another woman would enjoy the house they had planned for themselves.

She gave a slight shrug and looked round when Kyle came back into the room bearing a tray with large coffee pot and delicately formed china cups and saucers which seemed incongruous to Jan in the rugged gran-

deur of the room. What had happened to the man-
sized brown earthenware mugs he had once liked? No
doubt he had smashed them into a thousand pieces, as
he had shattered her life.

'Will you pour, Elena?' he requested in a manner
that took for granted her willingness.

'Of course.'

He had set the tray on a low table before the sofa
and Elena sprang to her feet, her small capable hands
dealing expertly with the fine china. Lifting a steaming
cup intended for Jan, she said in a hostess-like voice:
'Would you like to sit here and have your coffee?' She
indicated a corner of the sofa, but Jan frowned.

'No, I'll sit here,' she said perversely, taking her cup
and sinking gracefully into the chair beside the fire,
conscious of Kyle's eyes on the new, maturer outline
of her figure beneath the white high-necked sweater
she wore under the loosened jacket of her suit. He had
himself removed the pile-lined suede jacket he had
worn earlier, and she noted that his body under the
red plaid of his shirt and dark brown corded pants was
as whipcord lean as ever ... perhaps more so. Certainly
his face had a harder look than she remembered, the
bones seeming to stretch the weathered skin to tautness over cheeks and jaws.

'Would you care for a cake—or a cookie?' Elena
passed an oval plate in front of Jan.

'No, thanks.' Food at that moment would have
choked her, and she had a sudden longing for Don's
reassuring presence.

'Well, I do see what you mean,' Elena prattled on,
offering the plate to Kyle where he sat at one corner
of the sofa, his expression unreadable. He refused the
food, but swallowed his first cup of coffee in one gulp.
'You *have* put on a little weight since ...' She let her
voice trail off tactfully, then frowned when Kyle said:

'You look very well, Jan. Being a—business woman
—suits you.'

Jan fought away the sinking feeling the sound of his

voice sent plummeting through her. She would have been less than human, she told herself, if those deeply masculine tones left her unaffected after what Kyle had meant to her once. Sharply, she pulled her mind away from the whispered words of love he had poured into her ears with that same voice ... words which must even now be captured in the solid walls of the room they had shared ... words she had thought he meant. Had the bedroom where they had loved been the first to fall under the annihilating destruction of the builder's hammer? She drew a deep breath and realised that she was the focus of two pairs of eyes, one pale blue, the other sombre dark brown.

'I—I enjoy my work very much,' she told them, and sipped the scalding coffee unfeelingly. Then she lifted her eyes to stare levelly into Kyle's. 'I'm very fond of the people I work with, too.'

The semblance of a bleak smile quirked one corner of his tightly held mouth. 'Especially the one who looked as if he was abandoning Daniel in the lions' den when you came into the house.'

'Don's been very good to me.' Her voice was lowered huskily. 'He was there when I needed help badly.'

'Finding men when you—*needed*—them has never been a problem for you, has it?' Kyle's insinuation came with such sudden candour that Jan's breath was expelled in harsh disbelief, while Elena smothered a small exclamation of satisfaction. Her triumph was shortlived, however, for Kyle turned sharply to her.

'Don't you have to get back to your place and meet the company buyer?' he voiced brusquely, his eyes so remote and hard that even Elena seemed cowed by them. She jumped to her feet and set her cup down with a clatter on the tray.

'Yes, I—I guess I'd better be moving along.' Her eyes flicked briefly over Jan. 'I'll no doubt be seeing you again before you leave, Jan.'

'Don't count on it.' It was an effort for her to control her tone after Kyle's scathing directness.

He walked with Elena to the door, helping her into her warm jacket and saying something to her in a low voice so that Jan missed the words, and suddenly she again felt deserted, as if even Elena's presence was more desirable than a tension-filled duo of herself and Kyle. She was on her feet when he came back with his easy stride to the fireplace area.

'I have to go too, Kyle. The men——'

'Stay where you are!' he almost barked. 'The men can wait a while for your company.'

Surprised, she sat back again in the chair, her eyes darkened to midnight as they fastened on his lean figure before the fire. The harsh lines had deepened round his mouth so that he looked much older than the thirty-two years she knew him to be. His next words startled her to wide-eyed amazement.

'What's Don McLeish to you?'

'Don?' She blinked, then remembered that Kyle no longer had any right to question her about anything. He had given up that right the night he had possessed her body without love, with no passion but that generated by hate. 'Don and I are going to be married as soon as possible after—after——'

'After you've divorced me?' His voice changed subtly as he leaned over her chair. Mockingly, he said: 'It's taken a long time for you to get around to thinking of divorce. Why, Jan?'

The effort required to remove her gaze from the fiercely burning glare in his eyes seemed to tire her, and her shoulders drooped as she looked into the fire beside them and said listlessly: 'For the same reason you've been putting off setting the wheels in motion so that you can marry—Elena, I suppose.'

He straightened and stood with his back to the fire again. 'What makes you think I want to marry Elena?'

Jan shrugged. 'It hardly needs two good eyes to see that's what she expects. She's—very much at home here.'

'Does that bother you?' he asked softly, his eyes mocking as hers glanced off them and back to the red glow of the fire. If she had been in any doubt about his reason for demanding her presence at Silvercreek, it faded in the light of that one remark.

'Why should it bother me?' she shrugged with unforced coolness. 'You and I mean nothing to each other any more—you made sure of that three years ago.'

A full minute of silence followed, time when Kyle said nothing though she was conscious of his eyes on the bent darkness of her severely styled hair. At last he spoke, so quietly that his voice was almost lost in the crackle of burning logs.

'I've always thought you were the one who did that.'

'You'll never believe any differently, will you, Kyle?'

'It's a long-ingrained habit of mine to believe the evidence of my own eyes,' he ground out with sudden harshness, then he abruptly changed tack. 'What happened to Paul? Did you throw him over too when you re-discovered McLeish?'

Jan made an involuntary exclamation, her eyes widening to something resembling pity. 'You didn't know—about Paul? He—he's dead, Kyle.'

'*What?*'

'I'm sorry ... I thought you'd have heard, somehow. You—you remember he was going to South America on an engineering job? His plane—crashed into a mountain. I'm sorry,' she repeated, genuine compassion for his shocked disbelief evident in her distressed eyes. 'I thought you must have heard ... known ...'

'No, I didn't know.' Kyle turned to face the fire, the leaping flames outlined the shadowed tautness under his cheekbones. His face seemed suddenly drawn, and Jan remembered again the deep friendship that had existed between the two men until ...

'When did this happen?'

'Not long after—six weeks after we—he—left here.'

She was unprepared for the bitter savagery of his attack as soon as the words left her lips, and she stared up at him aghast.

'You didn't give a damn for him either, did you? You used me to get what you'd always wanted in life— a name, a man you could twist round your finger. And when I found out the kind of no-good cheat I'd married, you battened on to Paul. It must have really upset you when he died,' he gritted, 'because that meant you had to look around for some other blind, idiotic male to stick your claws into!'

Swiftly, brutally, he reached down for her wrist and jerked her to her feet, their bodies touching as he twisted her arm behind her back and forced her against him. 'But, as I've said, that was never a problem for you, was it, wide-eyed Jan? Men always fall for that little girl lost look you've practised until it's perfect. Even now,' he muttered, his eyes raking the shocked contours of her face with its creamy skin, his body suddenly giving out its awareness of her full curves against it, 'I could——'

'Let me go.' Jan found her voice, though it came out with twisted dryness. 'I'm not alone now, with only your friend with a liking for sick jokes for protection! Don loves me, and when he finds out you've attacked me——'

'Attacked you?' Abruptly, Kyle let her go so that she staggered back to the chair and sat down suddenly as its edge touched the back of her knees. 'Oh no, Jan, I'm not attacking you—in a physical way. That would be too easy, wouldn't it? You never could resist the touch of a man's hand, or your power to make him forget everything except his desire for your body.'

Her eyes searched the unrelieved stoniness of his face. 'What is it you want of me?' she whispered. 'Why did you want me to come back here?'

His eyes were shaded as he turned his back to the fire and looked down at her shrinking figure in the chair, his shrug almost imperceptible.

'Who knows? Maybe I wanted to see your greedy little soul's reaction to the transformation of Silvercreek into the place you'd imagined ... the place you thought you would rule over as you did me.'

'You've made your point,' Jan said shakily, getting to her feet and sidestepping past him to make her way over the animal skin rugs and polished floor to the front door. Swift as a cougar he was behind her, and she looked up defiantly with one hand on the door handle. 'You, and Silvercreek House, stopped existing for me the night before I left here. So I wish Elena joy of you both.'

Kyle's hand came down to cover hers as she started to turn the handle, a pulse beating erratically at his temple when she turned to look back at him.

'I've told you it's not as easy as all that,' he said tersely, his arm still half encircling her waist as it reached for the door. Softly, his breath fanning across her skin with abrasive warmth, he went on: 'Did you really think I'd let you off that lightly, sweetheart? A nice quick divorce so you can do the same to some other man? No,' his eyes narrowed, 'you're going to stay here until you've learned a little lesson I've been planning to teach you for a long time.'

CHAPTER THREE

JAN's head reared back like a wayward colt's, her eyes fixing on Kyle's in glittering sarcasm.

'I've never taken you for a fool, Kyle, but that's what you are if you think you can keep me here against my will. There are four men out there who'd come running if I as much as let out one peep.'

Kyle was unruffled by the threat. 'And what would you tell them when they came running?' he drawled. 'That you got the vapours because your still loving husband begged you to come back to him?' His long arm made a wide sweep round the room. 'Even though he's gone to such a lot of trouble and expense to fix everything the way you wanted it?' His smile showed a mocking glint of straight white teeth. 'Don't you think they'd feel just the least bit sorry for me?'

Slowly, comprehension dawned in Jan's eyes. 'You've been planning this for a long time, haven't you?'

'A long time, baby,' he confirmed briskly, hardness coming back to his eyes. 'I'll admit I hadn't expected you to turn up with a full contingent of males to protect you—a stupid oversight on my part—but that might turn out to be for the best, now I think of it. It shouldn't be too hard to get rid of them once I've convinced them that you and I are going to work things out in our own way and in our own time.'

'You're crazy!' Jan burst out, backing away from him so that her shoulder blades felt the hard bluntness of wood behind them. 'Don would never——'

'Don will do exactly what he needs to do to keep his business going,' he dismissed curtly. 'Capital Films needs this job badly, and he's not about to see his company go belly-up after all the years he's put into it. Not even for your charming self.' He bowed sarcastically from the waist and Jan had a flashing urge to strike the strong outthrust of his blue-shadowed jaw. But the question that rose to her mind made her fist grow limp.

'How do you know so much about Capital? About me? Have you paid somebody to spy for you?'

'We can talk a lot more comfortably by the fire,' he said, ignoring her flashing eyes as he fitted his long fingers under one elbow to lead her there, but she snatched her arm from his grip and marched to the hearth area herself, taking the seat Elena had occupied. Kyle stood for a moment before the fire, then bent to add two more logs to the glowing ashes before settling himself in the chair opposite.

'To answer your questions—no, I didn't pay somebody to spy for me. I happen to have a friend who's acquainted with the film world in Vancouver. He knows who's doing what—how much and how little—as I'd know how well or badly a rancher is doing in my area. He didn't have to do much spying to know that Capital was on its uppers.' He crossed one leg over the other in a way that had once been dearly familiar to her, regarding the toe of his deeply polished boot with a frown between his eyes. 'As for you, I found out where you were by chance. Some time after my grandmother died, I was watching television—rare for me, but it was a Sunday. Anyway, I happened to see a documentary film on the film-makers—the one you appeared in, do you remember it?'

Jan nodded numbly. She hadn't wanted to be included in the footage, but Don had persuaded her that the glimpse of her making notes on an outdoor shot would be unrecognisable. But Kyle had seen and recognised her ... and set into motion his plan which had led her to sit opposite him before a cosy fire in the refurbished ranch house now.

'How long did you stay with Paul?' he asked quietly, conversationally.

She swallowed, feeling the dryness in her throat as an insuperable obstacle to speech. She had to answer his question carefully. If Kyle found out about Robbie's existence, he would have to be convinced that the child was Paul's, not his. Or did he already know, as he knew so much else about her life?

'A-about six weeks—until he went to ...'

Her voice trailed away, and the tightening of Kyle's jaw told her that he, too, was remembering the death of his friend. If only she could tell him that Paul hadn't betrayed that friendship, that there had been nothing between Jan and him except Paul's too-juvenile sense of humour. True, she had spent a few weeks in Paul's apartment in Vancouver while he stayed with his married sister nearby, but only until she found work to support herself in a place of her own.

It was Jan who persuaded Paul not to get in touch with Kyle as he had wanted to do. At that time, shock was still reverberating through her body from Kyle's ruthless exacting of revenge. The hurt accumulated in her heart from the years of not belonging to anyone was as nothing compared to the agony of knowing how little Kyle trusted her, how little their love had meant to him ... Remembrance of it brought Jan's mouth together into a compressed line, and she stood up jerkily.

'I have to see to dinner for the men.'

Kyle rose too in one lithe movement. 'You'll all eat here, of course,' he said smoothly. 'Hannah's already preparing a meal for six.'

Jan stopped on her way to the door and looked back at him. Dark eyes met violet blue with forceful intent, and she shook her head bewilderedly.

'You can't mean to go through with this, Kyle.'

'Can't I? Try me!'

'But what can you hope to gain by it? We don't mean anything to each other any more.'

'Haven't you heard that revenge is sweet?'

She turned back and walked to the door with bent

head, saying in a strangled voice: 'I thought you'd taken your fill of revenge on the last night I spent under this roof.'

The footsteps following her halted suddenly and she cast a glance over her shoulder to see Kyle's shoulders thrown back, his jaw tautened to whiteness. Then his shoulder line dropped and he moved towards her lazily.

'That was only a beginning, my darling,' he mocked. 'I used to call you that, didn't I? Darling ... dearest ... sweetheart ... love——'

'Stop it!' As if to shut out the sound, Jan threw her hands over her ears, but still the words reverberated in her head. Words he had spoken in the soft darkness of night, words that now held no passion or tenderness, only the clanging discord of hatred and mockery. Her hands were wrenched away from her ears with savage ruthlessness.

'Don't worry,' Kyle said grimly. 'I won't call you those things unless there's somebody I want to impress with our ecstatic reconciliation. I won't even touch you unless it's under the same circumstances. And that's going to be the sweetest revenge of all,' he gloated, releasing her hands but digging his fingers into the thick silkiness of her hair to pull her face closer to the blind fury in his. 'Because to a woman like you, being without a man is like an addict without his drugs, isn't it? You can't even last out three days—or should I say nights?'

It was at this point that Jan lifted her hand and struck him forcibly on the taut flesh of his cheek, her fingers showing white first against his tanned skin then turning almost instantly to red.

For a moment he stood stock still with clenched fists, which relaxed when he smiled without mirth and said: 'Thanks. You've just confirmed what I said—a woman doesn't strike out unless a man's getting too close to the truth.'

'And you're such an authority on women, aren't you?' she blasted, nostrils flaring.

'I've known my share of them. I was never a monk, exactly.'

'Only as far as Elena's concerned!'

Anger flared briefly at the back of his eyes, so that she knew she had hit home. 'Elena is—special.'

'I wish to heaven you'd discovered that before you married me!' Her eyes snapped as a thought came to her. 'What reason will you give her for my—staying on here?' Judging from their earlier encounter, Jan could visualise Elena's reaction to that piece of news.

'She'll accept whatever I tell her,' he shrugged arrogantly, then regarded her with appraising eyes. 'So you've decided to stay, my faithful little wife?'

'You haven't left me much of a choice, have you?' she said bitterly. 'The livelihood of four men depends on this job, and I can see it's a waste of time appealing to your better nature.'

'A complete waste,' he agreed, and glanced at the luminous hands on his watch. 'Should we say seven? Then we can have a drink before dinner.'

'I'll convey your invitation to the men,' sarcastically, stepping out into the already darkening afternoon while he held the door open for her.

'When are you planning on moving into the house?'

Jan lost her balance slightly as she twisted round to face his broad figure silhouetted in the doorway. 'What?'

'Unless you were thinking of bedding down in the stables when the team takes off, you'll need a roof over your head.' His dry tone changed to briskness. 'And I'd suggest you'll find it a lot more comfortable dressing for dinner here than in a cramped motor home competing for space with four men—although, of course, being in close proximity to men doesn't bother you too much, does it?'

The sarcasm in his voice brought a giant wave of hopelessness washing over her. The whole idea was impossible, ridiculous. She stepped back towards him in the half light, her eyes raised with unconscious pleading to his.

'Kyle, please don't do this . . . you must see how crazy it is to expect me to live here in the house with—with you.'

'What's so crazy about wanting my wife back where she belongs?' His voice, face and eyes held an implacable blandness. 'You play your part when you go over there right now, and I'll do my share tonight.'

'They'll never believe it, especially Don.' She racked her brains for other plausible reasons for not staying. 'I don't have clothes for an extended stay, and for another thing——'

'Your clothes are all here as you left them,' he returned brusquely, his eyes going calculatingly over her outlined figure. 'Most of them should fit you still.'

Shock rippled through her at the thought that the clothes she had worn during their short marriage, the ones Kyle's money had paid for, were still hanging in closets like ghostly reminders of the past. Had Kyle taken leave of his senses? 'What?' she asked faintly when his voice penetrated her consciousness.

'You were about to give me another reason for not staying here,' he pointed out with exaggerated patience.

'I—I can't stay, Kyle,' she said desperately. 'There's —someone I have to be with in Vancouver——'

'A male, no doubt?' he jibed, shaking his head when she nodded dumbly. 'You never stop, do you, Jan? What's this one's name? Tom? Dick? Harry?'

'Rob—Robert,' she stammered. 'I must get back to him within the week, he——'

'Sorry, sweetheart,' he clipped, 'he'll have to wait in line like the rest of us. Now if you'll excuse me, I have work to do.'

The door was closed suddenly in her stricken face, and she stared sightlessly at the cedar panels while thoughts raced chaotically through her brain. She had to get back to Robbie next week . . . any longer separation denoted, in her remembrance of a love-starved childhood, the abandonment she herself had known as a baby, a fate she had vowed would never happen to a child of hers.

But after a few moments of utter stillness on the porch, she turned and descended the steps to the path which would take her to where the motor home was parked some distance away behind a thick screen of pines. Calmer, she reasoned as she walked that Hilda was hardly one of the unfeeling foster-mothers she herself had known as a child. Hilda loved Robbie almost as if he was one of her own, and would care for him until his mother's return. But when would that be? she thought forlornly. How long would it take for Kyle to feel satisfied that sufficient revenge had been exacted?

Pausing at one corner of the stockyard, she leaned against the warm red of the barn and looked across the frost-encrusted yard to where the motor home blazed with friendly lights. Christmas would be a drear season for the men sheltering in the warmth of those lights if this assignment was not forthcoming ... a joyless one for them and their families if, instead of trimming a tree and searching for presents to put under it, they were forced to cut corners and join the many others looking for employment ...

Jan hesitated in the dimly lit corner of the galleried upstairs hall, looking down at the group of men gathered round the fireplace area with drinks in their hands.

Illogically, she frowned as their relaxed, occasionally laughing voices floated up to her. It was her own acting talent that had convinced them of her wish to give her marriage to Kyle another try. Only Don had taken her aside to question her sudden change of mind.

'If I thought this was prompted by a mistaken sense of loyalty to me and the men, I'd go over there right now and tell Kyle Masters what he can do with his job,' he had said with unusual ferocity, grasping her chin and forcing her to look into his eyes. 'Is this truly what *you* want to do, Jan?'

'Yes ... yes, Don,' she injected a note of eagerness into her voice. 'Seeing him again, and—knowing he wants me to s-stay ...'

Strangely, Don had not seemed surprised. 'I've wondered,' he nodded, though not happily. 'You've never seemed anxious for a divorce, and obviously he hasn't either, so ...' His eyes, soft with concern, looked gravely into hers. 'But if things don't work out, I want you to promise that you'll get in touch with me as soon as you need me.'

'I promise,' she had agreed shakily, and felt his hand tighten on hers until it hurt.

'Have you told him about Robbie?' he asked quietly.

'No,' she said with frightened quickness, then, seeing his questioning lift of brows, explained hurriedly: 'There won't be anything—between us. This is just a time to—talk, see where things go. It would only complicate matters if I told Kyle about Robbie now, then we decide that it's no go.'

'There is that possibility, then?'

'Oh yes, yes, of course,' she had assured him quickly ... too quickly, perhaps, because when he looked closely into her eyes it was as if he saw to the depths of her. Down to the truth she had been trying to deny to herself. Kyle's touch, even in anger, still had the power to send shockwaves like an electric current through her entire body ...

Now while she looked down at Kyle and Don as they stood slightly apart from the others in seemingly serious conversation, she reflected wryly on the universal instinct of men to put up a front of apparent amity on a social level, whatever their differences might be.

Kyle had changed into a dark blazer jacket and charcoal slacks, the white polo neck of his sweater contrasting sharply with the darkness of his hair and skin. His dress was casual, but beside the thick sweater and light blue slacks Don wore he looked like a man on his way to the most elegant restaurant in town. Even John French, still in his jacket of well-cut cashmere, paled to insignificance ... an observation which would have mortified him had Jan voiced it, accustomed as he was to his place as sartorially perfect in any group.

The heads of all five men swivelled round to the stairs as Jan moved down them in her knee-length dress of scarlet velvet, the one she had thought to wear for the mock Christmas dinner film for Timberline. As Kyle had told her, everything she had left in the huge bedroom they had once shared was still there, hanging in the closet like inanimate wraiths of happier times. Drawers holding her sweaters and lingerie still sent out a faint waft of the lavender sachets she had used.

But her fingers had been trembling before they reached for the drawers and closet doors. She had braced herself before reaching the room for the changes she expected to see, sure that Kyle would have started his reconstruction there, and had stood frozen inside the doorway as she realised that not one thing had been changed. As if she had left it for only a few moments, the room looked ready to receive her with its widely welcoming poster bed covered with the hand-stitched spread which had lain over three generations of Masters, including Kyle and herself. She had stared at the coverlet, memories rushing through her and leaving her trembling until she forced her eyes away to the rest of the room, seeing the familiar placing of honey-toned maple dressing table and Kyle's tall set of drawers. Putting her in this room was a refinement of cruelty she had not expected, even from Kyle.

Her throat had closed over at the thought that came to her then. Did Kyle expect her to share this room, this bed, with him? No ... he had said, and sounded sincere in his avowal, that he would not touch her except to convince others of their reconciliation. But that could have been an insincere promise made to lure her into the mad arrangement he had thought up. Would his method of exacting vengeance involve more of the same treatment he had meted out on her last night here?

This thought shadowed her eyes as she reached the bottom of the stairs to where Kyle waited for her, the expression in his deep-set eyes obscured in the soft lighting of the room. She knew that the vivid scarlet of her closely fitted dress outlined every curve of her figure, although the neckline came demurely to just below her throat, but she could detect no hint of admiration or condemnation in his expression.

Of the group around the hearth, only Don's head was averted towards the fire; the others looked expectantly, even hopefully, across the expanse of living room to where Kyle greeted her in a purposefully carrying voice. There was no doubt in Jan's mind that he had very successfully laid the grounds for making her staying on plausible.

'You're more beautiful than ever, Jan ... there's just one thing I'd like to change, if I may?'

Without waiting for her answer, his hands reached up behind her head and loosened the tight coil of glossy black hair so that it fell in soft waves round her face and shoulders, slipping into his pocket the hairpins he had removed so deftly.

'That's much better,' he said softly, this time as if for her ears alone, and his fingers slid down her arm to clasp her hand and draw her across the floor.

The other men evidently agreed with him, and said so in varying degrees of enthusiasm as she sat on the sofa and accepted the sherry Kyle handed to her before seating himself beside her and taking her free hand casually in his, tightening his grip imperceptibly when she made a move to pull away.

'Jan's beautiful however she wears her hair,' Don said abruptly from his stance beside the fire, the heavy-lidded look of his eyes as they went over her telling Jan that he had drunk more than one of the straight whiskies he now held in his hand.

'You won't get any arguments from me on that score,' Kyle agreed smoothly, and seemed deliberately to stroke with his thumb against the slim gold band he had placed on her finger so long ago. His voice lowered to impressive huskiness when he added : 'And it isn't just a surface thing with Jan ... her beauty goes all the way through. I was a fool to let things go wrong between us. Believe me, I've regretted every minute of wasted time.'

Like a palpable thing, Jan could feel the sympathy of the team, apart from Don, flow towards Kyle and she turned the dark violet of her eyes up to meet the brown of his, half believing the sincere-sounding break in his voice. For a few moments his eyes held blankness as they returned her look, then she turned her head sharply away when a gleam of irony flitted across their depths.

'Mind if I help myself to a drink?' Don asked heavily, and Kyle waved a hand towards a small padded bar in the far corner of the room.

'Be my guest. You'll excuse me if I don't get up right now, won't you?'

Don appeared to take in his implication that he hated to leave Jan's side even to offer hospitality to his guests, and his brow lowered like a thundercloud as he passed near them. John followed him to the bar and Kyle, who seemed to have drunk little of the whisky from his glass on a small table beside him, concentrated his attention on Hank and Bernie.

'I've seen quite a lot of your work on television,' he charmed, 'and I must say that I admire your skill with a camera. I'm just hopeless—remember, honey?' He turned to Jan as if expecting her to join him in reminiscing, as if things were already sorted out between them.

'Yes, I do,' she replied sweetly. 'It always surprised

me that you were so skilled in some areas and absolutely hopeless in others.' Like faith and trust, she wanted to add, but there was reward enough for now in seeing the newly shaven line of his hard jaw tighten to paleness.

'There's really nothing to it, Kyle,' Hank said in a friendly, eager way, then launched into a detailed account of how to take family pictures with this or that camera, and made it all sound very difficult indeed. Kyle, however, managed to maintain his expression of interest, even when the talk spilled over into the meal they shared shortly after in the wood-panelled dining room.

Jan had little choice but to accept the place Kyle allotted her by pulling out the chair opposite his own at the head of the table, thus making it look more than ever as if they were a happily married couple entertaining friends.

The middle-aged Indian woman who served the meal silently was strange to Jan, and she wondered what had happened to Sarah, the ill-tempered housekeeper who had been Esmeralda Masters' closest ally in her campaign against Jan. But whatever Sarah's failings had been, she was an exemplary cook, which the silent Hannah obviously was not.

John, from his seat on Jan's right, leaned over to whisper: 'Might have been better if we'd dined Mexican style after all,' when thin vegetable soup was succeeded by meat which should have been succulently tender but had been roasted to tough dryness.

'Maybe she's a mistress of desserts,' she whispered back with a conspiratorial smile which faded as her eyes met Kyle's down the length of the table. Her breath was pulled in and held in her throat at the loathing she saw there. Like an insect pronged by a pin her gaze was caught and held by the raw feeling in those eyes until Kyle removed them from her with cold deliberation and returned his attention to Hank.

A shiver of icy dread ran over Jan and she felt an

intense longing to be with Don, to hear the voice that had reassured her so many times before in moments of despair. But it was not until the men were beginning to make a move towards the door that she had a chance to speak privately with him, and she realised then that there was no way she could unburden herself to him this time. Not unless she wanted to deepen the frown on the face now looking down into hers as they stood just beyond the fireside area.

'Don't look so worried, Jan,' he smiled, only his mouth making the gesture. The eating of food, no matter how badly cooked, had sobered him considerably, and there was a regretful tenderness in his brief stroking of a finger over her cheek—a gesture Kyle, standing near the door with the other men, didn't miss, she noticed. But her only thought now was one of panic at being left alone with him. 'You're doing the right thing,' Don went on. 'I came down here with you because I wasn't sure of what Kyle's motives were in asking that you come alone to make the arrangements.'

'But now you're sure?' Without meaning to, Jan betrayed her sudden spurt of anger and Don looked at her thoughtfully, pausing before answering.

'I'm sure of one thing,' he said finally, his eyes reaching behind her to Kyle, who had turned his back to them. 'Kyle Masters cares very deeply for you, and he bitterly regrets what happened between you.'

'Is that what he told you?' she asked tightly.

'Not in so many words, maybe, but I know men pretty well, Jan, and that one loves you.'

But he doesn't, Jan wanted to scream. He just wants revenge for his hurt pride, a vent for the hatred he's been nurturing for nearly three years. Oh Don, how could you be taken in by his smooth talk of regret, his implication that the house had been refurbished with the specific aim of winning me back, when all the time he was motivated by vengeful spite ... a spite he'll start exercising the moment you step through that door tonight. But she said none of these things, and became conscious that Don's eyes were fixed on hers again.

'In all fairness you have to give it a try, Jan. He's promised he won't force you into anything you don't want, and I believe that or I wouldn't be leaving here tomorrow morning without you.'

Jan was startled out of her bitter line of thought to say: 'Tomorrow morning? You—you're leaving?'

Don nodded soberly. 'He's given us permission to film the logging operations before the snow comes, with the proviso that we don't use the footage if he changes his mind about us doing the film at all.'

'Leaving the onus on me?' she asked flatly. 'If I don't—come up to scratch—the whole deal's off, is that it?'

For a brief moment Don looked uncomfortable, and she wondered, shocked, if Kyle could have been right in his estimation that Don would do whatever he had to do to keep Capital on its feet—even to sacrificing her.

'What's changed you so suddenly, Jan? You're acting as if you're being forced into this, yet before dinner you seemed anxious to give your marriage another try. You know I wouldn't leave you here if I didn't think it's what you want yourself deep down, what you've always wanted. And you have to admit,' he smiled bleakly, 'it would be the perfect answer for Robbie, to have two parents who love him.'

Was she imagining that note of his pushing her into something against her will, persuading her by means of her son that it was the right thing to do? Her eyes searched the familiar fair-skinned face, but read nothing there except seemingly genuine concern.

'Yes,' she sighed, turning away partially, 'it would be the perfect answer.' Swinging back as the thought struck her, she asked in a low voice: 'You didn't tell Kyle about—Robbie, did you?'

'Of course not. That's for you to do if and when the

time is right.' His broad hands came up to clasp her upper arms. 'He does care about you, Jan,' he said quietly, his eyes going round the magnificence of the room they were in. 'Look at all he's done for you. It must have cost a minor fortune to have all this carried out away out here.'

'It's easy to spend money when you have it,' she pointed out bitterly.

'And it's when you don't have much that it becomes so important,' he countered, his lips tightening.

Jan knew suddenly that her suspicions of his motives were unfair and unjustified. For the first time she noticed the lines of strain round his eyes, lines which would have been more readily noticeable on a darker-skinned man. Selfishly, she had been concerned mainly with his apparent willingness to abandon her to Kyle's mercies, while to Don she was only part of the problems facing him. He had the responsibility for the welfare of loyal employees, as well as an understandable reluctance to let the business he loved slide away into nothingness.

Impulsively she reached up and kissed his cheek lightly, not caring whether Kyle saw the gesture or not. 'Don't worry, Don,' she whispered huskily, 'things will work out in the right way—they usually do, in the end.' Except for Janice Brown, she concluded silently, but there was no trace of this self-pitying thought as she walked with Don to the door where Kyle and the other men waited. Yet a flurry of panic at the thought of being left alone with the husband who hated her made her address Don directly.

'When will you be back?'

He turned his head in surprise, looking swiftly at Kyle's inscrutable face before coming back to Jan. 'Didn't you know? We'll be back again close to Christmas for the family celebration thing—unless circumstances dictate differently,' he added heavily, his meaning clear as his eyes met the inexpressive brown of Kyle's.

'But you'll have to come back this way from filming the forest operation!'

'Evidently not,' Don told her drily. 'There's a logging road that will get us back on the main highway and save quite a few miles over rough territory.'

Jan had a very good idea that it was Kyle who was behind the time-saving short cut on the team's return to Vancouver, and she turned away after saying a shaky goodbye to the men. She shivered as she halted behind the sofa and leaned her weight on its back as if needing its support.

'You're cold, Jan. Come closer to the fire.'

Instead of the gloating expression she had expected to see on his face, Kyle seemed introspectively preoccupied, almost as if he had forgotten she existed.

Nevertheless, it was obvious he had no trouble in detecting the trace of dread in her voice when she stammered: 'No ... I—I think I'll go to b-bed.' Why, oh, why had he put her in that room of all the vacant bedrooms at Silvercreek House?

'Nonsense,' he returned briskly. 'It's early yet, and there's a perfectly good fire to enjoy.' As he spoke he moved towards the bar in the far corner and she shrank away from him, thinking his intention was to lead her forcibly to enjoy the fire with him. Impatience tinged his voice, and a look that was partially obscure in the deep recesses of his eyes combined to send a series of tremors through her body. 'I've told you I have no designs on you physically, so relax and drink the brandy I'm about to pour for you.'

Refusal sprang to her lips as his tall figure brushed past her, but she bit it back. Perhaps the fiery warmth of alcohol would quiet the apprehensive fingers clenching her stomach muscles. She crossed to the fire and sat shivering in the armchair to one side of it, the glow from half-spent logs lending colour to her paled cheeks. She had no real wish to go up to that bedroom yet, in any case. Her most recent memory of it from those far-off days was still one that chilled, deadened those parts of her that had responded so joyously to Kyle before that last night. Parts of her which had remained in frozen dormancy since then, in spite of Don's patient efforts, in spite of her own almost desperate attempts to unlock the door to which only Kyle had the key.

She glanced up warily as he approached the seating area, two generous servings of dark amber brandy in balloon-shaped glasses in his hands.

'Why did you give me—that room?' she asked constrictedly as she automatically accepted the glass he held out to her.

'Would you rather share mine?' he countered drily, settling himself in the corner of the sofa nearest her chair.

'You don't——?'

'No,' he smiled sardonically, 'I haven't used that room for quite some time. So don't panic—I'll only sleep there by my wife's invitation.' He stared down into the dark brown liquid and swirled it slightly in his hand.

'I'm sure Elena won't bother with engraved invitations,' she said tartly, taking a deep swallow of the burning spirit and scarcely feeling its sting although in normal circumstances she hated the smell, the taste, the effect of brandy.

'I wasn't thinking of Elena particularly,' he returned slowly, then raised his eyes to look meaningly into hers. So meaningly that Jan took another gulp of brandy before replying.

'If you're thinking of an invitation from me, you can forget it! Do you really think a woman's turned on by being kidnapped and blackmailed?'

His voice was silky, smooth. 'You've sent out invitations without those incentives, and I haven't forgotten how well we got along once upon a time. Don't you remember, Jan? Here in front of this fireplace——'

'Not this fireplace,' she choked, rising hurriedly to her feet and looking down at him loathingly. 'Can't you accept that it's over, done with, finished? What we had between us died three years ago, Kyle—why prolong the agony with this revenge thing? I mean nothing to you apart from an object you extract revenge from because of that stupid pride of yours——'

'Pride isn't stupid to me!' In one movement he rose and twisted her arm behind her back, bringing her body into close—too close—contact with his. Suddenly his face bore the same imprint of savagery that must have been stamped on the primitive peoples who had trodden this land long before he had. Written there was the unheeding desire to keep that which belonged to him, whether it be land, material possessions, or a woman. For a moment the hard leanness of his body against her, the male scent of him beneath the civilised veneer of after shave and tobacco from the cigars he smoked, made Jan's senses reel. Dizziness overwhelmed her, not just from the familiar arousal of her senses from their body contact, but from something much deeper than she had ever recognised before. A depth that reached back to the beginning of time and made everything unimportant except the being together, the union, of one man and one woman ...

'Let me go, Kyle!' Frightened by the turn her thoughts had taken, Jan struggled to be free, only to find herself more tightly bound to that steel-clad figure of potent masculinity. Sobbing, she gasped: 'All I want to do is to live in peace with my—with Rob——'

'With your Robert?' Suddenly she was released, so precipitately that she staggered and almost fell on the thick darkness of bearskin under their feet. Kyle's face had paled under the weathered copper of his skin. 'This Robert really gets to you, doesn't he?' he put softly, yet his eyes held steely disregard for her distress. 'Does Don know about him?'

Jan drew a quivering breath. 'Yes.'

'Yet he's content with the crumbs you throw him, like the peck on the cheek you gave him tonight? What kind of man is he?' His tone conveyed his own opinion of Don's masculinity.

'Don't you dare say anything about Don!' she flared, pushing her free hand against his chest but not succeeding in breaking away from him. Instead, his grip on her other wrist tightened and sent crushing pains waving up her arm. 'He—he has more kindness and—and understanding in his little finger than you have in your whole body!' A broken sob broke from her. 'You're hurting my arm.'

He released the pressure slightly but continued to hold her against him. Like a shutter falling before his eyes, contempt faded from them until they looked neutrally down at her.

'Do you sleep with him?'

Jan stared back at him, speechless. There was nothing in his expression to suggest that he cared one way or the other, and it was this more than the bold question itself that added extra fuel to her anger.

'Even if that was any of your business I wouldn't tell you,' she snapped, angry colour flooding her cheeks and emphasising the fiery sparkle of her eyes.

'That probably means you don't.' Unperturbed, he gazed steadily down at her. 'And how about Robert? Are you more generous with your favours there?'

Fury lent impetus to the words she threw at him half hysterically. 'Of course! I'm generosity itself where he's concerned. I can't wait till work's over so I can get back to him—we live together, you see. Didn't your spy tell you that too? I spend every free minute I have with him—the evenings, weekends, and the nights— they're best of all——'

The breath was knocked from her when he released her suddenly and pushed her away from him so that she collapsed into the chair behind her.

'Don't you want to hear all the details, Kyle?' she mocked against his silence. 'You seem interested in my love life, so——'

'Go to bed, Jan,' he bit off harshly, then turned stiffly away to pick up his glass still half filled with brandy.

Still shaking from the emotional storm that had

ripped through her, she stared at his broad back for a moment or two then got unsteadily to her feet. Kyle stood with rock-like stillness as she walked across to the stairs, but when she looked from half way up he had thrown himself on to the sofa, his head tipped back as he raised the glass to his mouth.

CHAPTER FOUR

WEARINESS, physical and emotional, made Jan fall asleep with merciful quickness in the high, wide bed in the master suite. Oblivion and the stillness of the Cariboo covered her for nine hours, and when at last she blinked and came awake reluctantly she sensed the lateness of the hour.

Sliding out of bed, she went across to the heavy drapes covering the window to the front of the house and pulled them aside to look out to where the ranch buildings lay to her right beyond the trees.

The cream-coloured motor home and the mobile van were gone, as if they had never been there. An air of isolation hung over the red-painted structures, bringing the knowledge that Kyle and his men had moved out too over the frost-encrusted ground stretching in every direction around the ranch house.

What must the silent Hannah be thinking of the boss's wife, who had turned up after an absence of three years to ostensibly resume her position of mistress of Silvercreek House? Surely Kyle must have realised that the house staff and ranch hands would talk, would wonder, would speculate?

Pushing aside her irritation, Jan showered in the yellow-tiled bathroom adjoining the master bedroom and donned the thick white sweater and hip-hugging jeans she had brought with her. Not for anything would she delve into the dresser drawers still filled with fine wool and warm thick Indian Siwash sweaters she had left behind.

She halted abruptly on her way down the wide staircase to the living room below. Sunlight struggled to edge past the heavy draperies, still drawn, at the front windows, and the room looked exactly as it had when she left it the night before, except that the dying embers of the fire had been enclosed by a steel mesh screen— presumably by Kyle before he had gone to bed. Either Hannah was as bad a housekeeper as she was cook, or she had not turned up for work at all this morning.

This last conjecture proved to be true, as a cryptic note from Kyle on the kitchen table informed her. 'Jan —Help yourself to what you need. Hannah has been called away to her family. I'll be back before dark. K.'

Too parched to spare time for indignation, Jan filled the coffee percolator and plugged it into the outlet on the long counter adjacent to the stove, glancing round the kitchen with eyes that were no longer shocked at the changes she found—changes she herself had envisioned.

The old cupboards had been torn out and new ones of satin-finished hardwood installed, the ones separating kitchen from dinette area fronted with amber-coloured glass showing the distorted outlines inside of glassware and serving bowls. Stove, fridge and upright freezer were finished in a deep copper colour which blended perfectly with the gold counter tops and copper-bottomed pans hung from hooks near the cooking area. On the floor, easily cleaned vinyl in pale gold led to the utility area near the back door, where bright new washing and drying machines in the same shade of copper were installed.

A woman's dream kitchen ... *one* woman's dream of a kitchen, Jan corrected herself, swallowing a lump in her throat. A kitchen Elena would enjoy when she came here as Kyle's bride, a domain his first wife had been denied because of the pervading presence of Sarah, who had been a better cook than Jan could ever aspire to be. Could Elena cook? Did it matter? No doubt there were a dozen Hannahs willing and eager to work in the boss's house as his cook.

Jan crossed over and searched in the cupboards close

to where the coffee was sending out its pungent fragrance. Ah! Kyle hadn't disposed of the earthenware mugs—there they were, brown and glistening with cleanliness, at the rear of the china cupboard behind the delicate china cups Elena favoured. There was almost an air of defiance in the way Jan took one of the mugs from the cupboard and poured the aromatic coffee into it, wandering then to the broad window above the sink unit to look out on the lake beyond lawns still white with crusted frost.

The lake, wider than a river, narrower than an inlet from the sea, was enclosed on either side by dark-hued pine trees sweeping down the hillsides to hug the edges of the lake with an aura of protectiveness. Acting as a funnel, the lake opened out at its far end to hilly pasture country that stretched for miles into the blue distance where white-capped peaks rose from purple-smudged mountains beneath them.

A tug of happy remembrance made Jan blink and turn away from the view she had loved, the one she had had no difficulty in conjuring up at any time during the intervening years ... A glimpse of Kyle's note on the table, his decisive handwriting, stiffened her spine and compressed her full lips as she poured a second cup of coffee. Not for a second did she believe that Hannah had been called away at a time most convenient for Kyle's purposes ... more likely he had sent her away in fear of her learning too much about the falseness of this reconciliation and babbling her knowledge to the rest of the Silvercreek employees.

But no—fear was the wrong word to apply to Kyle. He feared nothing and no one; he was master of his own destiny and those whose livelihood depended on him. The men who worked for him held him in almost worshipful regard—a fact that had once deepened her own love for him—and not one of them would challenge his right to do things his way. And, sighing, Jan had to admit that Kyle's way was usually the best in the long run. Except where his marriage was concerned ...

She stared thoughtfully at the note he had left, and slow fury rose to check her breathing when realisation was borne in on her speculative mind. His motive for leaving her alone in the house was to force her into a housekeeping role which he knew would turn the knife in the wound he was inflicting by making her stay here. How much satisfaction it would give that streak of cruelty in his nature to have her meekly wait on him, cook his meals, clean his house! A satisfaction he would never know, she told herself determinedly, pushing aside the dirty dishes he had used for his breakfast—a breakfast he had obviously cooked for himself—and throwing two slices of bread into the toaster. She would do nothing but clean up after herself . . . he could do what he liked about his own mess.

After eating the toast, spread liberally with the golden honey she found in one of the cupboards, she fastidiously washed up her own plate and coffee mug, then went upstairs to make the bed she had slept in, ignoring the still drawn curtains in the vast living room and the air of staleness from last night's cigar and cigarette smoke.

The bed was soon made, the task performed with an automatic precision that left no room for thought or memory, and then she hesitated in the middle of the room. It was all very well for her to thwart Kyle's plans for her subjugation, but what was she to do with herself during those long hours when he was away? Brood about her situation—about Robbie? The barrier she had erected against thinking of her son crumbled suddenly, and tears shimmered in her eyes as she gave way to her longing to hold the sturdy little body against her . . . so tightly that he would rebel against her confining arms as he had yesterday morning. Yesterday! Already it seemed a year away, and the days stretched emptily before her until she would see her child again.

Her breath drew in on a strangled sob when the idea came to her that she could at least phone Hilda and perhaps even speak to Robbie. Almost before the thought formed she was rushing from the room and down the wide staircase. Stumbling in the gloom at the bottom, she ran across and jerked wide the curtains, blinking as blinding sunlight cascaded in golden shafts to caress the faintly dusty gleam of polished wood floor. Swallowing hard and sniffing, Jan crossed to Kyle's study where the phone must still be, staring in stupefied silence at dark panels that resisted her entry. Her trembling fingers rattled the handle impotently and she cried out her frustration. He couldn't have! Not even Kyle could be that cruel!

But a few more desperate tugs convinced her that he had indeed locked the office door. Despair coursed through her as she leaned her head against the unyielding door and gave way to helpless tears. Not even Capital's team of fine men was worth this, she cried noisily, to be cut off even by phone from the one person in the world she cared about.

Drained of thought and feeling, she lay against the door. But inevitably her brain came into action again and she stiffened suddenly. The main house telephone had been the only one when she had lived here, but Kyle had spoken many times of having one installed elsewhere on the ranch for the use of the employees. Probably it was at Tom Henderson's house—although he was a bachelor in his fifties, Tom was ranch manager and as such rated a house instead of a section in the single men's bunkhouse.

Racing upstairs, Jan tore one of the thick Indian sweaters from a drawer, pulling it on as she rushed down again and let herself out of the back door in the kitchen's utility area. She was glad of the sweater's chunky warmth for, although the sun fell unstintingly from a blue sky, the air was cold and the ground still frozen hard under her feet. But she was scarcely aware of that as she approached the belt of trees separating the main house from the rest of the ranch, following the pine-needled path at a half trot until she came out to the neat row of employee houses situated opposite the working area of the ranch.

Her brows came down in a frown as her eyes noted the uncanny stillness, the air of abandonment about the small bungalows. Where were the wives, the children too young to be sent away to school? Hysteria rose like a ball to her throat. Had Kyle sent all of his employees away as he had despatched Hannah? But how could he run a ranch of this size without help?

Fear took the place of puzzlement as she looked round the deserted area with panicked eyes. Had Kyle been so driven by thoughts of revenge on what he thought a faithless wife as to have slipped over the boundary of normalcy into an unknown world of his own?

She started violently when a voice shouted 'Jan!' from one of the high-roofed barns some distance away, then relief swept through her as she recognised Tom Henderson's stocky figure coming rapidly towards her, a smile wreathing his leathered features as he came closer.

'Jan! It's good to see you!' His deep voice filled with pleasure as he enfolded her in a bear-hug of breathtaking intensity. Then he held her away from him, narrow brown eyes glistening suspiciously. Huskily, he said: 'I knew you'd come back one day. You and Kyle belong together just like the moon and stars do.'

'You're getting poetical in your middle age, Tom!' she teased, forcing a breathless laugh as she disentangled herself from his short but powerful arms.

'Heck, no!' he disclaimed modestly, running his gaze more closely over her. 'It's just that I've known Kyle since he was a little boy, and he's never been the same since you left. I can tell when he's hurting. Why *did* you leave, Jan?' he asked quietly at last, taking a step back and regarding her with sobered eyes.

'Kyle—didn't tell you?'

Tom shook his head without taking his eyes from hers. 'Nope. I asked him just once, thinking he'd maybe like to talk about it, but he bit my head off and told me to mind my own business. It's never been mentioned between us since, but——' He seemed embarrassed as he went on doggedly: 'I've always suspected it had something to do with that friend of his, Paul whatever his name was. Was he involved, Jan?'

'In a way,' she admitted slowly, not wanting to put the blame on Paul when the basic cause of the separation was Kyle's mistrust of her faithfulness and loyalty. 'But that was all a long time ago, Tom,' she reminded him softly, and he nodded agreement, a less exuberant smile lighting his features.

'That's the truth! And now everything's going to be fine. Already Kyle's like a new man—or should I say like the man he used to be?' he twinkled.

'You saw him this morning?'

'For a minute or two before he rode out with Tiny and Shortstop.'

Mention of the two ranch hands brought a half smile to Jan's lips. How often had she laughed with Kyle about the seemingly mismatched pair—Tiny with his ponderous bulk and Shortstop with his wiry agility seeming unlikely friends and partners but never to be seen far from each other. Single men.

'What's happened to everybody, Tom?' she asked, waving a hand towards the bugalows. 'The place seems deserted.'

'Didn't Kyle tell you?' he asked, obviously surprised, then a chuckle lightened his chesty voice. 'Guess you had more things to talk about last night than the expenses-paid second honeymoon Kyle's sent the married men on! They'll be taking in a few of the shows and rodeos in New Mexico, of course, but that was mostly Kyle's cover for giving the men an extra vacation. They've worked hard, and Kyle's had a good year.'

'I'm glad,' she said insincerely, half turning away then looking back at Tom's ruggedly contented face. 'By the way, something seems to be wrong with the phone at the house—could I use the other one?'

'The other one?' he puzzled slowly. 'There's no other phone, Jan, don't you remember?'

The light laugh Jan gave sounded unconvincing even to herself. 'Oh ... I must have misunderstood Kyle. I thought he said——'

'If you'd like me to come up and have a look at it,' Tom suggested, 'I'd be happy to, though I don't know too much about phones and such like.'

'It's not important,' Jan assured him hastily. 'I—I'll try again a little later. Thanks, Tom.'

'If you need anything, just give me a holler,' the manager called after her. 'Kyle said I was to——'

'I have everything I need, thanks,' Jan waved back, quickening her step as tears threatened to overwhelm her again.

Kyle must really hate her if he had gone to the trouble of sending most of his men and their wives away on an expensive junket to New Mexico in order to keep her in isolation at Silvercreek House, retaining only the men he knew would be loyal to him to the point of stupidity.

But keeping her cooped up, a virtual prisoner without even the use of a phone to contact the outside world, would give him little satisfaction she vowed as she stamped her way into the kitchen. A few days of coming home to a cheerless, uncleaned house and no warming meal cooking on the stove would alter his opinion of his own wisdom in keeping her here against her will.

Jan was sitting on the broad window seat in the master bedroom, hugging her knees as she watched the sun disappear behind the sparsely clad hills to the front of the house. Steeped in lethargy, she heard no sounds of Kyle's arrival home until the bedroom door burst open and he stood there, one hand still on the knob as his furious eyes met the slow turn of hers from the window.

'Tired, darling?' he jeered, pushing the door violently away from him as if wishing the inanimate wood was Jan's flesh and striding across to stand over her with unconcealed anger in the greyness of his face. 'I can see from the state of the house that you've been working like a slave all day.'

'It was your choice to send Hannah away,' she replied dully, dropping her gaze from the lines of tiredness edging his mouth and eyes. 'You didn't tell me that I was expected to be your slave as well as your prisoner.'

'You're neither my prisoner nor my slave,' he whipped at her downbent head. 'I haven't shackled you in chains or confined you to bread and water, have I?'

'You didn't have to do that, did you?' she threw back bitterly. 'All you had to do was set me down in the middle of the wilderness and cut off access to a phone.'

'So that's it,' he said softly, and was silent for long moments, though she felt his eyes on her head in quiet contemplation. Then: 'I always lock the study door when I'm out for the day, because the stockmen's pay is kept there in the safe.' The words were an unhurried statement of fact, not an apology.

'Pay for stockmen who are off on a second honeymoon in New Mexico?' she flashed hotly, jerking her head back to look scathingly at his marble-hard eyes.

'Oh yes, Tom told me he'd seen you.' Kyle bit his lip and continued to regard her steadily, though he changed the subject abruptly. 'Are you planning on starving us to death?'

She shrugged. 'I'm not hungry.'

'Well, I am,' he said grimly. 'Unlike you, I've been working like a slave all day, and you might remember that I'm not my sweetest self when I'm—hungry.'

His deliberate pause brought sudden wild colour to her cheeks in an agony of remembrance of another hunger of his ... the urgent need to express the deep smouldering passion in his roused body, the desire to be one with her, his wife. Her eyes went automatically to the wide bed behind them and she heard his mirthless chuckle.

'I see you do remember. How far back does your

memory go, sweetheart?' His silky voice was in direct
opposition to the savage jerk which brought her to her
feet with a suddenness that made her stagger against
the unyielding hardness of his chest and gasp as his
arms came round her in a steely grasp to hold her there.

'Does it go back as far as this?' Strain had put an edge
into his voice, a coolness he seemed to dredge from
deep inside him. But there was nothing remotely chilly
in the sudden warm seeking of his lips at her ear, her
eyes, the wildly pulsing deep hollow at the base of her
throat, her softly moulded chin ... 'Or this?' he said
thickly over the shocked parting of her lips, possessing
them a second later with no regard for her whispered:
'No, Kyle, no!'

Only a few moments were lost to numbed awareness,
stretched out moments when she became painfully,
pulsingly, conscious of the familiar thrust of his body
against hers, the sweetly pungent odour of honest sweat
mingled with the scents of horse and tobacco, the
overwhelming urge to curve her own body to the
forceful outlines of his. The harsh abrasion of his
day-old beard lacerated the tender skin surrounding
her mouth, but she felt no pain ... just a heightened
response to this visible sign of his aggressive masculinity.

And responding she was ... mindlessly, heedlessly.
As if sensing her need to slide her hands round
his neck, Kyle loosened his grip on her arms, thrusting
impatiently under the loose folds of her sweater to
caress her warm skin and send shivers of wanton delight along her nerve ends. His hair was crisp and thick
between her fingers, the feel of it as well known to her
as the firm column of his neck which her finger tips
explored a moment later.

Time rushed away from her, as if there had been no
hurtful span between now and when she had lain with
Kyle on this bed before ... that she was on the bed she
knew from the sinking softness beneath her, the hard
demanding man's body above her. And now where his
rough-skinned hands had caressed his mouth followed,

making her aware that her sweater and bra had somehow been removed, leaving the creamy swell of her
tender flesh open to his seeking lips. But she didn't
mind ... didn't care. A small voice at the back of her
brain told her that she should protest, resist, but ...
dear God, how often had she dreamed of just this
moment, when her own need was answered by the equal
longing of her husband? Kyle ...

'Kyle?' she whispered, reaching up with her hands
to draw him back when he lifted his head, his breath
laboured as if he had been running a long distance.
'Oh Kyle, I need you so much ...'

Her eyes had fluttered closed, containing within her
the wild joy coursing through her veins in the knowledge that Kyle needed, wanted her as much as she
craved his touch on her body which had been dead but
was now gloriously, singingly alive. Filled with the
deep rapture of it, she failed to sense the stiffening of
his body against her until his weight lifted abruptly.
Her eyes flew open to see him standing by the bed, his
eyes flicking contemptuously over her from the hol-
lowed indent of waist to the soft fullness of parted
lips and unpinned black hair streaming across the
white bedspread. Her eyes snapped open in disbelief
when his voice lashed her with the sting of a whip.

'I bet that's what you tell all the boys!' he mocked,
then leaned over her until his head was only inches
from hers. Savage cruelty etched the outline of his face
in the dimmed light. 'I have to make a correction. I
was wrong in my estimate of how long you could wait
for a fix for your addiction.'

Disbelief faded, and the rush of anger replacing it
brought her hands up, her fingers curved with the
intention of scratching that knowing, satisfied look
from his face, but his movement was even faster, his
hands clamping round her wrists at the same time as
they lifted.

'Easy now,' he jeered softly, forcing her hands back

until they lay at either side of her face. 'You might need me even more before you leave here, and I doubt if my tender heart could let you go cold turkey that long.'

'Heart? You don't have a heart,' she gasped, choking on a sob as she fought a losing battle against the tears filling her eyes.

'I did have one once, don't you remember? In fact, if you were to thumb through your collection of used hearts some time you might find that the deadest and driest of them all belongs to me.' He straightened abruptly. 'That's right, have a good cry but don't wallow in it. I'll expect you downstairs in an hour to eat the dinner I'll throw together myself.'

'Oh, go away!' she cried brokenly, pulling the bedspread across her nakedness and turning her head into the pillows, closing her eyes though tears still found their way through the dark-lashed lids and crept down her face. 'I'll never eat anything your hands have touched!'

The ensuing silence was so profound that she wondered if he had gone, crossing the thick carpet on soundless feet, but then she heard him move, his voice coming to her as he skirted the end of the bed and made for the door.

'You'll eat it,' he said grimly, 'even if I have to carry you down and force-feed you.'

She heard the sharp click of the door behind him, and sobs immediately rose up to emerge as hoarse gasps from lips that still held the imprint of his on their swollen surfaces. How could she have been so stupid as to fall into the trap he had woven for her? Every glance, every word he had spoken to her, had made it more than clear that he still believed she had been a willing participant in that scene played out in this very bedroom nearly three years ago. The hurt to his pride had intensified, magnified itself to such immense proportions that it had turned back on itself to eat away at his innards until its poison could even stop the desire he had felt for her at its most consuming moment—something he would never have been able to do—once.

And he had desired her. She knew that with as much assurance as she knew every crease in Robbie's baby skin, every inch of his sturdy flesh, every nuance of expression that spoke of his father. His father ... a sob of hysteria strangled in her throat at the irony of Kyle's assumption that Robbie was yet another of the men whose hearts she strung like beads on a necklace. If he ever found out ... but he must never find out that she had borne him a son.

If Kyle knew about his son, he would move heaven and earth to get him and keep him by his side. And what would it do to Robbie to be brought up by an embittered man who hated the woman who had given the boy birth?

Shuddering, Jan pulled down the bedspread to a point just below her shoulders and turned further into the pillows. Thoughts that were too painful to examine were expunged in the blessed unconsciousness of sleep ...

CHAPTER FIVE

'Jan? Wake up, Jan ... it's time to eat!'

Stirring with a moan of unwillingness, Jan blinked and stared up at the man's tall figure by the bed. Kyle, she discerned hazily, but a Kyle subtly different from the one who had left the room earlier. In the soft glow thrown by the bedside lamp, she saw that he had shaved and changed into a light checked shirt of lemon and white, his dark brown hair brushed neatly to one side as if he had recently stood under a cleansing shower. Or was the change she detected due more to the less harsh cast of the eyes looking down into hers? She put an unconscious hand up to smooth back the hair from her face and felt the cool wetness of fresh tears on her cheek.

'I'm—not hungry,' she said in a voice made husky by sleep, turning her face away from the light to hide her ravaged face from his penetrating stare.

'I'll wait ten minutes while you freshen up,' was his unrelenting response, an underlying hint of steel suggesting that he would not hesitate to carry out his earlier threat of feeding her forcibly if she refused to comply.

Jan lay for long minutes after he had gone from the room, steeling herself to rise and force her unwilling feet down the stairs to where Kyle waited with the meal he had prepared. A meal he was determined she would eat whether she wanted to or not.

Too weary emotionally to contemplate further resistance, she rose at last and slid out of her jeans before crossing to take fresh underwear from the dresser drawer. The mirror there reflected hair tousled and tumbling over creamy shoulders, eyes heavy-lidded from the tears she had shed, a mouth tremblingly vulnerable, and breasts firm and tilted as if awaiting the love Kyle had cut off so abruptly. With an incoherent exclamation, Jan turned and went to the closet, pulling out a wool pants suit in a shade of blue which leapt to meet the colour of her eyes.

The eyes she bathed quickly in cold water to lessen the swelling, and a few deft touches of make-up brought her face to a reasonable facsimile of its normal appearance. Her hair she tied back loosely with a white chiffon scarf, having no time to arrange it in its customary style of sophisticated neatness.

But although she was only two minutes over the time Kyle had specified, he had one foot on the bottom stair as she started the downward trip. He said nothing, however, simply watching her with an enigmatically veiled look in his brown eyes before stepping back and indicating the kitchen when she came to a step where she was level with his eyes.

'I've set it up in the kitchen. I'm not much on organising a pretty table in the dining room.'

'It doesn't matter,' she said lifelessly, following his broad shoulders and tapered hips into the kitchen where he held open the door for her and waved to one of the two places set at the square table. Only a flicker of surprise disturbed her numbed expression when she saw the gold and white check of a gingham cloth he had spread there, the sparkling crystal of wine glasses edging the neatly laid cutlery and cloth napkins to match the tablecloth.

'Sit down,' he told her tersely over his shoulder as he went to take two plates from the copper-toned oven, cursing softly and reaching for a cloth when the heated plates scorched his fingers. After placing Jan's plate unceremoniously before her, he dumped his own and disappeared in the direction of the cellar, rattling noisily down the stairs in his search for wine to fill the goblets.

Jan was still staring bemusedly at her plate when he returned with a bottle of dark red wine. A steak that spoke more of the toughened hide of a very old cow instead of the succulent rib beef which it was lay shrivelled at one side of the plate, while pellet-like peas, insufficiently cooked from their dried state, shared the rest of the space with diced carrots suffering from the opposite problem.

'So I'm not much on cooking either!' Kyle snapped, extracting the cork with a savage twist of his wrist and standing beside her to splash wine into her glass before sitting down opposite to pour his own.

Fighting against a vague feeling of compassion stirring deep within her—how could Kyle be considered pathetic in anything he did?—Jan said the first thing that sprang to mind. 'You used to cook the fish you caught very well.'

His eyes met hers over the glass he had raised to his lips, and he took a mouthful of wine before saying: 'Cooking over an open fire is a lot different from using that damn stove.' He glared balefully at the shining appliance, then picked up his knife and fork to tackle the leathery steak. 'Anyway, it's all we have, so eat.'

He seemed to feel the steadiness of her gaze on his bent head, and looked up with an impatient jerk of his head. 'I said——'

Ignoring that, Jan said slowly, in a voice of discovery: '*You* cooked the meal last night, didn't you? Hannah only served it.'

Kyle's jaw clamped tightly and he looked down at his plate. 'Does it matter who cooked it? It might not have been up to your usual standards, but at least it offered you and your friends a little amusement.' His eyes flicked up to hers again, and she knew he was remembering the smile she had shared with John French at the dinner table.

'No one would have been amused if they'd known you had cooked it yourself. On the contrary, you'd have gained a lot of mileage in your campaign to have them

believe you—needed me.' Jan's lips twisted in bitterness
at the last words, the ones she had used to him just over
an hour ago in the bedroom above. 'What could be
more touching than a man having to cook a meal for
guests after working hard all day?'

Kyle chewed on a section of meat which seemed tough
going even for his strong teeth. At last he said: 'On the
other hand, I could have lost points if they thought I
wanted you back just to cook and housekeep for me,
so'—as if he had given the matter careful prior con-
sideration—'I decided it would be better to let them
understand I wanted you for your physical charms
alone. Not that those aren't considerable,' he added
with sarcastic hastiness, his eyes dropping from her pale
cheeks to the rounded curves of her breasts before
coming back to her flashing eyes. 'There's something
different about you, you're more——' He hesitated and
narrowed his eyes.

'As Elena pointed out, I've put on weight,' Jan
snapped, resenting the feelings those probing eyes
aroused more than the catty remark of the other girl.

'No, it's not that,' he shook his head, seeming puzzled
now. 'You even feel different ... but then,' he smiled
briefly with his mouth, his eyes remaining hard, 'they
say experience broadens a person.'

Choking, Jan rose to her feet with a scrape of the chair
legs on the vinyl floor. 'You—you never give up, do
you? If you think I'll stay here for weeks until you make
up your mind to let me go, you're mistaken, Kyle
Masters! I'd sooner be eaten by a bear out there than
put up with your insults—film or no film!'

'Sit down,' he said mildly and, surprised, she sat,
but stared balefully across the table at him, her eyes
dark blue pools of contempt. 'For one thing, black bears
such as you're likely to find around here don't take to
human flesh, and for another ...' He looked at her
consideringly, then seemed to come to some sort of
decision. 'This—Robert seems to be pretty important
to you at the moment.'

Jan's breath drew in sharply and she looked down at the blood red wine in her glass. 'He'll always be the most important person in my life,' she said in a lowered voice, then lifted the glass and swallowed convulsively on the wine, missing the white clenching of Kyle's fist across the table. Her head came up in a quick movement, however, at the clipped hardness of his tone.

'All right, I'll make a deal with you. You take care of things around the house and cook the meals, and I'll allow you the use of the phone—in the evenings when I'm home.'

The brightness faded from Jan's eyes when she heard his last condition for the deal. How could she make a call to Hilda and ask after Robbie with Kyle hovering in the background, no doubt listening to every word she uttered? But at least it was a concession ... the only one she was likely to get, judging from the hard jut of Kyle's jaw as he applied himself once more to the food before him.

'Tonight?' she asked, her fingers twined painfully together on her lap.

He shook his head negatively and swallowed with difficulty on a piece of meat which was not only tough but cooled by now. 'No. Tomorrow evening when I'm satisfied you're able to fulfil your part of the bargain. Now eat.'

And surprisingly she did, hunger taking precedence over distaste for the unappetising meal in the knowledge that tomorrow she could at least find out how Robbie was, and even speak to him if she called early enough before he was put to bed.

Maybe she could even stick it out for a week or two until Kyle's lust for revenge was satisfied, until Don and the other men had completed their filming and so secured the company for the time being at least. All she needed was a contact, however remote, with her baby son ...

All the next day Jan sped busily round the house, her

happiness pivoting round the thought of the evening phone call to Vancouver. Filling the hours till then proved no real hardship because the furniture in the house called out for the deep polishing it had obviously missed for some time, the rugs needed shaking in the brisk brightness of crisp air, the floors brought to their original gleaming softness with the aid of a buffing machine which Jan found in a cupboard in the utility room.

Kyle's last brusque words the night before had been: 'Leave the fire, I'll do it when I come home,' but Jan had used the pent-up store of energy from yesterday's idleness by clearing the massive grate and re-laying it ready for the strike of a match. The brass fire accessories had been polished to burnished brightness, every speck of dust removed from the hearth stretching in a wide platform from beyond each side of the yawning fireplace itself, before she retired to the kitchen to bake the apple cinnamon pie she had prepared earlier and set about preparations for the meal she had planned for Kyle's return.

Not that she was doing it for Kyle's benefit, she reminded herself as she spooned marinade over the round roast she had taken from the freezer first thing. But mingled with the joyous anticipation of phoning Hilda that evening had been the determination to show Kyle that his revenge motive for bringing her here was back-firing in the surest way possible. That she had enjoyed the day's cleaning and scouring was evident in the cared-for look of his possessions, the bright face she would present to him the minute he came in the door. He could derive little pleasure from knowing that his captive enjoyed her confinement to hearth and home, to the cooking and cleaning she would have carried out in a loving way if things had been different.

Jan wandered across to gaze mistily from the kitchen window to where approaching evening had already begun to descend beyond the lake. If things had been different ... if Robbie had been playing round her feet

right now, waiting for the daddy he idolised to come
striding through the door to toss him high in the air
with arms bronzed to supple strength ... if he turned
then to kiss her, his lips warm and hard, the deep glow
in his eyes promising ...

She started violently when the back door opened
suddenly, the soft wistfulness still clouding her eyes as
she glanced round from the window. There was no
way she could adjust her expression instantly, and she
knew that Kyle would recognise that look in her eyes
and mock the regretful longing he saw there.

But it was Elena, not Kyle, who stood with her back
to the closed door. She had thrown back the hood of
her blue jacket, her short fair curls framing a face
attractively reddened from the icy air outside, her eyes
sparkling with health and something else that could
have been malice. Without invitation, she sauntered
over in high-legged riding boots and perched on the
edge of the table.

'Isn't it customary to knock around here when you're
invading someone's privacy?' Jan asked drily.

Elena shrugged. 'Most people around here don't have
anything to hide.' Her insolent tone implied that Jan
had unmentionable secrets to preserve. 'Besides, this
house has been a second home to me all my life. Old
Mrs Masters always made me welcome ... you might
say I was like a granddaughter to her.'

'Really? Then it's a pity for you and her that Kyle
never brought himself to make that relationship
official!' Stung, Jan turned her back on the other girl
and took the golden-brown double-crusted pie from the
oven, closing the door quickly against loss of heat to
finish cooking the roast.

'Don't think you can get Kyle back by displaying
the kitchen skills you've acquired since you left here,'
Elena snapped back, her face flushed a deeper pink
when Jan swung round to face her. 'And just where did
you pick up such skills, anyway?' she insinuated.
'Taking care of all the stray men in your life?'

'Of course, where else?'

Jan's cool reply seemed to flummox Elena for a moment, then battle lit in her eyes again.

'Kyle's not that stupid, to be taken in by your cheap looks and pretend innocence again!'

Jan's brows rose in polite enquiry. 'Are you suggesting that he's stupid in any degree?'

'Kyle's been stupid only twice that I know of,' Elena returned deliberately. 'The first time when he married you without seeing you as the scheming money-hungry nobody you are; the second when he brought you back here. I told him it was foolish to settle the divorce details here instead of in a lawyer's office!'

'Divorce?' Jan's eyes widened in the pretended innocence Elena had accused her of a moment before. Part of her basically honest nature hated what she was about to do, but scruples were torn aside in the overwhelming rush of memories concerning this vindictive woman and the older one who had made her life misery during her short marriage to Kyle. 'That certainly didn't seem to be what Kyle had in mind last night.' She even managed what could have been construed as a maidenly blush which was brought about more by reflected heat from the oven than modesty.

'You're lying!' Elena hissed, but her eyes held a brief flash of uncertainty.

'Am I?'

Jan heard the outside door open with Kyle's typical thrust, and she turned her back on Elena to walk across to him, hoping that distance and the shadowed light in the utility area would hide any shocked expression in his face.

He had undone the zipper on his heavy brown jacket, his hands suspended then on his chest as Jan approached him. The wariness in his eyes gave way to grim understanding as he glanced over Jan's head to where Elena sat tensed on the table's edge. A dry smile quirked at the corners of his mouth when Jan took

a too obvious deep breath before sliding her arms round
under his jacket.

'I thought you'd be home long before now, darling,'
she breathed huskily, her face lifted to his but her
eyes avoiding the ironic smile in his gold-flecked ones.

'You know I wouldn't stay away a minute longer
than I had to, sweetheart,' he said in a voice loud
enough to carry to Elena's ears, then he bent his head
to take her softly parted lips under his, his arms reaching round her in eloquent proof of his need to crush
her to his body.

Knowing the kiss was meant as no more than a
token, Jan accepted the possession of her lips passively.
Her mind was occupied with the other things about
him. The brisk coldness from his skin, the inevitable
roughness of his chin at this time of day, the sweet
scent of hay and horse on his clothes ...

And then she realised suddenly that this was no
fleeting or perfunctory token for Elena's benefit. It had
gone far beyond that, she realised, feeling her brain
begin to reel dizzily as his lips probed sensuously, inti-
mately, with a passion he would never have displayed
in front of another person at one time. Dear God, what
was he doing? Trying to provoke Elena to jealousy,
and using her, Jan, to do it?

Then she forgot Elena, forgot everything as her
treacherous body leapt in a glad response that recognised no artificial barriers her mind might impose.
Her hands were flat against the warm dampness of his
hard back muscles, then her fingers clutched convulsively at his shirt.

It was then that he released her, as if his purpose
had been accomplished. A mocking smile quickly replaced passion in his eyes as he shrugged out of his
jacket and hung it in the boot room just inside the
back door. He emerged tucking in his shirt ostenta-
tiously before reaching an arm round the stunned Jan
and walking casually over with her to the equally
shocked Elena.

'Hi, Elena,' he greeted easily. 'I hadn't expected to see you over here so soon.'

Jan felt a reluctant admiration for the fair girl, who recovered her equilibrium far sooner than she herself could. Jumping down from the table, she said coldly: 'Obviously not!'

Ignoring that, Kyle enquired mildly: 'Did you ride over? Pity. If you'd driven you could have stayed to dinner with us—what is it, honey?' he turned to Jan with a smile—'it sure smells good! But as you're riding,' he went on without waiting for an answer from Jan, 'you'd better leave right now or you won't get home before dark.'

'Don't worry, I'm going,' Elena snapped, and brushed past them, pausing before Kyle to look at him contemptuously. 'You're a fool, Kyle Masters!'

'Am I?' he returned evenly, then dropped his arm from Jan's waist. 'I'll see you to your horse.'

He ignored Elena's snapped: 'Don't bother!' and went to put his jacket on again. The beginning remorse in Jan grew cool when she saw that Elena, far from spurning Kyle's offer, waited for him at the door. Neither of them looked back at her as they went out.

Almost unaware that she did so, Jan sank into one of the kitchen chairs and stared vacantly into space. She had scored off Elena far more effectively than she could have dreamed, but the victory was like ashes in her mouth. The other girl's faithfulness to Kyle over long years, even during his marriage to another girl, had to prove something. Reluctantly, Jan concluded that that something must be a deep and true love capable of withstanding any setback. Except that display of marital passion she had witnessed a few minutes ago.

Was that why Kyle had insisted on going with her? Was he now explaining why it had happened, that he had merely been teaching his erstwhile wife a lesson? —a lesson he had brought her back as a virtual prisoner to undergo whether she wanted to or not!

Minutes ticked by, snippets of time that added up to a considerable slice as Jan waited for Kyle's return. What could be taking so long? Were his arms round Elena now, his lips pressed to hers as they had been to Jan's a short time before? And why shouldn't they be? Jan thought angrily as she rose in a jerky motion and went to turn on the heat under the pans of prepared vegetables on the stove. Some degree of intimacy must have developed between Elena and Kyle during the long reconstruction on the house. They had been alone together much more completely than she and Kyle had ever been. No vindictively possessive grandmother, no eagle-eyed Sarah to disturb that togetherness.

Kyle's face, when he returned a few minutes later, gave no sign of what might have transpired with Elena out at the stables. After a quick glance, Jan kept her head averted, busying herself with the warming of plates and bowls for their meal.

'Have I time to shower and change before dinner?' Kyle asked quietly behind her, and she swung round to see him indicate the creased and dirty state of his dark denim jeans and lighter blue shirt.

'Oh—yes. Dinner won't be ready for another half hour or so.'

Still he made no move to go, his eyes probing hers as if seeking the answer to a question that puzzled him. At last he spoke.

'What was the idea behind that little display?' he asked quietly, holding her gaze with his.

'Display? What display?'

'Oh, come on,' he exclaimed impatiently. 'The loving wife act in front of Elena.'

'Oh, did it bother her?' The innocent-eyed act was coming much more easily to her now, a fact that left her feeling uncomfortable with herself in a way she had never experienced before.

'If it didn't bother her, it bothered me!'

'Really?' Jan sounded delighted. 'Then I've learned

one part of my lesson from you very well! I'd never have believed how right you were.'

'About what?' he put tersely.

'Why, that revenge is sweet, Kyle. It really is,' she marvelled.

His jaw tightened to an angry line, but he said no more, spinning on his heel instead and taking himself with rapid strides to the door into the living room. Only the momentary pause of his boots indicated that he had noticed the polishing and scouring she had done that day.

Biting on a lip that threatened to tremble alarmingly, she followed a few moments later and was kneeling before the fire, watching the flames she had brought to life leaping up to consume the dry logs, when Kyle came downstairs again.

'I told you I would see to the fire,' he said quietly, then like a figure of darkness in black shirt and close-fitting pants, he went to the bar with his easy stride. 'What will you drink?'

'Sherry's fine,' she matched the coolness of his tone and turned back to the fire, supporting herself on the wide hearth which would soon be too warm to be near.

'It wasn't necessary for you to make my bed either,' he commented noncommittally as he handed her a fine-stemmed sherry glass, taking his own straight whisky to sit at the other side of the fireplace, his lean figure settling comfortably into what was obviously his favourite armchair.

'But isn't that a housekeeper's job?' Innocence again! She slid along the slate hearth away from the heat and lifted the sherry to sip it contemplatively. Nothing in her submissive outward demeanour revealed the heart-shaking moments she had spent in his room that morning. One opposite her own, smaller than hers, had proved the most difficult of all the rooms she had tackled that day. What would Kyle think if he knew that she had pressed her face to the pillow that still

held the indentation of his head, the faint scent of his
hair, the cologne he used ... His response would probably have been one of mocking satisfaction.

'You think I brought you here to be a housekeeper?'
he asked, his controlled tone speaking volumes for the
underlying spurt of anger in him.

'Wasn't that what you said? That I was to cook and
keep house for you in return for a nightly phone call
to——'

'To your Robert,' he agreed grimly, tossing down the
remainder of his drink and getting up to cross to the
bar for a refill.

'To my Robert,' she confirmed gravely. So what if he
continued to believe that Robbie was the latest in a
stream of lovers? Better he should think that than
guess at the truth. She looked up in quick apprehension
as he came back and reseated himself. 'You'll fulfil your
part of the bargain, won't you? I've kept mine ...'

'Oh yes, you've kept your end of it,' he agreed bleakly,
the eyes he cast round the room missing nothing of
the gleaming brass, the winking reflection of the fire in
tenderly polished furniture. 'You can phone your
Robert,' he swung his gaze back to her, 'after dinner.'

'Oh—dinner!' Jan sprang to her feet and rushed into
the kitchen where pots bubbled happily on the stove
and potatoes in their skins baked complacently beside
the roast in the oven.

'You haven't finished your drink,' Kyle's voice came
from behind as her fast-moving hands busied themselves over the pots. She turned abstractedly to take the
stemmed glass from him, scarcely feeling the warm
touch of his fingers against hers as she turned back to
the stove.

'Will you carve the meat, or should I do it out here?'
she asked absently as she opened the oven door and
removed the tenderly baked roast and set it on top of
the stove in its dish.

'I'll do it out here as there's only the two of us.'

Their eyes met as he reached for the roast, Kyle's moving away first when he pronged the meat on to the dish Jan had warmed for it.

'I'll—see to the gravy,' she said constrictedly, conscious now of the movement of her hands over the vegetable pans as she used their liquid to make a rich, dark brown gravy.

'I didn't know you could cook,' Kyle told her a short time later when they sat not far from each other at one end of the big table in the panelled dining room. It had seemed so ridiculous to lay places at opposite ends, so far from each other, that Jan had compromised and set them opposite each other at one end of the oval.

'I learned to cook at a very early age,' she said quietly, helping herself to cut green beans and passing the dish over to him. 'One of my foster-mothers thought it was a skill girls should learn—so they could keep their husbands happy,' she explained blandly, not meeting his eye. 'Unfortunately, my husband had no need for my cooking skills.'

Now she looked at him and saw the lines of his jaw draw together. 'You never mentioned that you'd like to—spend time in the kitchen,' he accused.

'Did I have a choice? Sarah ruled the kitchen as much as your grandmother——' She broke off and bit the soft part of her underlip before going on quietly: 'What happened to Sarah?'

He frowned and looked down at his plate. 'I—she retired just after my grandmother died.'

'Oh. And you've been taking care of yourself ever since?' The incredulous note in her voice brought a faint smile to his mouth.

'No. Jack Fowler's wife, Carol, has been coming in to see to things, and——'

'Elena, of course,' Jan interrupted quickly. 'She must have seen to your—needs?' Her dark brows arched in pretended enquiry.

'Her skills don't lie in the kitchen,' he countered with perfunctory dryness, pouring gravy liberally over the rarely done meat and beginning the meal as if unable to wait a moment longer.

'I suppose not,' Jan said thoughtfully, attacking her own plate with sudden hunger, adding brightly: 'Well, you can't expect one woman to have all the virtues, can you?'

'I suppose not,' he repeated her own words sourly, and remained silent for the rest of the meal except to say quietly, but with obvious sincerity, when Jan brought coffee to the table: 'That was a lovely meal, Jan, thanks.'

If he noticed that she had used the brown earthenware mugs for their coffee he made no sign of it, but finished the first and asked for another before Jan looked eagerly at him.

'May I make my call now?'

Kyle gave a barely perceptible sigh, but nodded: 'Of course. You've kept your end of the deal, so I'll keep mine.' The thought seemed to afford him little pleasure, however, as he rose and stacked their dishes to take into the kitchen.

'Could I have the key to the study?' Jan hated the sound of her own obsequiousness, but knew she had to have word of Robbie whatever the cost. Kyle's laconic reply left her staring in dumb amazement after his broad-shouldered figure as he went out of the room with the dishes.

'The door's been unlocked all day.'

CHAPTER SIX

ALL day ... all day ... the words echoed in her mind, anchoring her feet to the polished wood floor of the dining room. Instantly she wanted to scratch Kyle's eyes out, to flay him unmercifully for ... for what? For leaving the door unlocked, knowing that she wouldn't even try the handle after yesterday's fiasco? Or was it that he had trusted her to keep her word?

Still she trembled with anger. She could have called Hilda, spoken to Robbie, without Kyle's overweening presence in the background!

Tightlipped, she stalked across the hall to the study, where the door yielded at once to her pressure although it swung only partially back over the thick rug covering the room from wall to wall as she pushed it behind her and marched to the phone on Kyle's desk. Books lined every wall except the short one behind the desk where a filing cabinet and steel safe stood side by side, but Jan saw only the black shape of the telephone as she hurried across the room.

The Svensen phone seemed to ring for ever before the receiver was picked up, but at last Jan heard Hilda's querying: 'Hello?'

'Hilda? It's Jan.'

'Jan? Oh, how glad I am to hear your voice!' The muffled sound of Hilda's whisper to Johann that it was Jan on the line brought a reminiscent smile to Jan's lips.

'Hilda? How is——' she paused, lowering her voice to a hoarse whisper. 'How is Robbie?'

'Oh, Jan, I'm so glad you have called, we have such trouble here——'

'What's wrong?' Jan forgot the necessity for secrecy

and raised her voice to a pitch slightly higher than normal. 'Hilda, is something wrong with Robbie?'

'With Robbie, no,' Hilda returned worriedly. 'But——'

'What? What is it, Hilda?' Something of Jan's desperation got through to the other woman, and she seemed to pull herself together.

'Jan, it is Pieter, our little Pieter ... he has had an accident with a car.'

'Oh, no!' Jan's horror carried over the line, and Hilda said reassuringly:

'He is going to be all right, Jan, but he will be in the hospital for a long time. He has——' her voice broke off for a whispered consultation with her husband, '—it is crushed pelvis.'

'I'm so sorry, Hilda, I wish there was something I could do to help.'

'The biggest help is for you to take Robbie, Jan.'

'Take Robbie?' she repeated blankly.

'Jan, I am sorry, but it is impossible for me to care for him while I spend lot of time at the hospital with Pieter,' Hilda explained apologetically.

'But—but I can't bring him here!' Jan cried desperately, realising too late how selfish her words sounded. Hilda didn't, couldn't, know the circumstances of her forced stay at Silvercreek, and a faintly accusing note crept into the other woman's voice.

'Robbie is your child, Jan. I love him, but you must take care of him for now.'

'I know Robbie's my responsibility, Hilda. I—I'll think of something, but give me a little time. No—no, it's all right, I'll take care of him. You shouldn't have that worry as well as Pieter. I'll be in touch as soon as I can. Goodbye, Hilda.'

Jan replaced the receiver with trembling fingers and thought for a few moments with head bent over the desk. Kyle would have to let her go, let her go and take care of her son and perhaps help Hilda in such a time of trouble.

A slight sound from behind made Jan turn hurriedly towards the door, her eyes widening in horror when she saw Kyle wedged oddly against the frame, his face drained of colour.

'Kyle!'

Like a man sleepwalking, he pushed himself away from the door and came towards her. 'Robert's—a *child*?' he asked through grey-tinged lips. '*Your* child?'

Jan could only nod dumbly and watch with stricken eyes as he came near and leaned heavily with his hands on the desk top. For an endless minute he gazed sightlessly down at the outline of his long fingers against the dark wood of the desk, then he raised eyes filled with anguished question to Jan's.

'Whose child, Jan? Who is his father?'

Her mind whirled. She mustn't—ever—let him know that Robbie was his son. Because then he would take Robbie away from her, leaving her alone in a void bigger than the one she had known in her childhood. But now he was shaking her, his fingers making gouges in the soft flesh of her shoulders.

'Whose child is he, Jan?' he persisted starkly, and when she stared at him with blank eyes shook her again and questioned hoarsely: 'When was he born? How old is he?'

'Two,' she croaked, answering the last question first. 'He—he was born in—in October. He's——'

'Paul's child.' Kyle's hands dropped from her shoulders and lay lifelessly at his sides.

No, she wanted to scream, he's *your* child—from the shape of his fingernails to the curve of his little toes, he's your child. But she couldn't. Loving Robbie— needing him as she did—she couldn't risk losing him to Kyle. Kyle, who stood as if defeated, beaten, beside her. She couldn't bear that either.

'Kyle,' she whispered, 'I'm sorry, I——'

'It doesn't matter.' Brushing aside the words of apology, words which might have led to an open acknowledgement on Jan's part, he pulled himself together with visible force and said in a brittle, businesslike way: 'What's the problem? I gather there is one with the people he's staying with.'

Jan looked at him in wordless agony for endless moments until he gave her an impatient glance, his nostrils flared slightly as if the control he displayed cost him dearly.

'They—their little boy is in hospital, a car accident. Hilda wants me to take Robbie away because she can't cope with him as well as visits to Pieter.'

'He'll have to come here.' No prevarication, no indecisiveness, simply a bald statement of fact. Jan could see that his mind was already engaged on methods of transporting Robbie from Vancouver to Silvercreek.

'No!' The word burst from her in an explosive gasp. 'It would be better if I went back and——'

'And what?' he snapped, seeming to see her for the first time. 'Where could you take him that would be better than right here?' His brown hand reached for the receiver and handed it to Jan. 'Phone these people back and tell them we'll pick the child up tomorrow.'

'Tomorrow?' she stammered, staring up at him uncomprehendingly.

'Tomorrow,' he confirmed adamantly, adding in an abstracted way: 'Tom can fly you in and bring you back. I have to attend to other business in the morning.'

'Fly?' she questioned stupidly, her eyes fastened on the hard dark brown of his.

'Fly,' he confirmed again drily, clarifying for her obvious bewilderment: 'We have an airstrip here now, and Tom and I are qualified pilots, so you'll be quite safe. It brings civilisation a lot closer and minimises the awkwardness of situations such as we have now. I'll talk to Tom while you phone.'

Before Jan could collect her scattered senses, he was gone. She stared numbly at the receiver he had thrust into her hand, wondering if she could take the risk of bringing Robbie here, and knowing that once again she had little choice.

Jan glanced across at Tom's ruggedly set face above the controls, thankful that the plane's noise precluded conversation, and in knowing that the kindly ranch manager would not risk waking the child sleeping against her breast by shouting above the roar of the engine.

The older man had looked impassive all day, from their first taking off at ten until now when they were approaching the ranch on their return. He had asked no questions, made no comment apart from a silent raising of shaggy eyebrows when he had first seen Robbie. Jan had known without words from him that he saw the marked resemblance to Kyle in the boy's dark hair and eyes, in the steady look Robbie gave him when Tom lifted him in his arms to carry him to the taxi waiting below. What had Kyle told him? There was a bond between the two men which went back to Kyle's boyhood, so it was entirely possible that Kyle had confided in the man who had been like a father to him. A father!

Jan turned her head away to look down at the steeply carved hills and wide valleys passing beneath the four-seater plane, thinking again of how close she had come to telling Kyle the truth last night.

To her surprise he had followed her into the kitchen after the fatal telephone call, picking up a towel to dry the dishes she washed with shaking hands. His face still held a greyish tinge round his mouth, his eyes were bleak above the strongly defined nose, but the task was performed in silence until Jan was giving the counter and sink a final wipe with a dry cloth.

'I'll pour a drink,' he said, his voice as lifeless as his eyes. 'We have to do a little talking.'

Before she could make an objection, he had gone with a stride less forceful than usual into the living room, and when she followed him there a few minutes later he was standing staring contemplatively into the fire, his hand curved round a stubby whisky glass.

'Kyle, I'm tired. I—I think I'll go to bed,' she murmured, and thought he hadn't heard her, but at last his head lifted and turned. The breath seemed suddenly to be knocked from her body at the glimpse of bleak misery she saw in his eyes.

'You might as well have the drink before you go,' he inclined his head to a tall glass on one of the side tables. There was nothing in his attitude to suggest that he cared one way or the other if she drank it, but Jan hesitated for only another moment before sitting in one of the armchairs and lifting the glass.

Did the misery in his eyes mean that he had wanted Robbie to be his son? Even though he hated the mother? Any doubts she might have had as to his finding and taking Robbie no matter what faded as she looked up at the chiselled hardness of his profile, the unyielding thrust of blue shadowed jaw.

'It must have been a shock for you when—Paul was killed,' he said at last without looking at her. 'Was that why you went back to McLeish?'

Jan swallowed a threatening lump in her throat. 'Don was very good to me when I needed him.'

'Didn't it occur to you to ask me for help?' he asked tightly, throwing her a tortured glance. 'Paul was my friend.'

Paul! For Paul he would have helped her, not from any love for herself. 'And Don was mine,' she pointed out quietly. 'You had made it very clear that you never wanted to see me—or Paul—again.'

Kyle sat down suddenly on the coffee table before the fire, his features lit to flickering brightness in its reflection. 'At least Paul was able to give you something I obviously couldn't.'

'I—I'm not sure what you mean.'

An impatient jerk snapped his head round. 'A child —a son. I didn't do very well in that department, did

I? Paul accomplished in a matter of weeks what I couldn't in six months!'

Appalled, Jan stared at the profile he had turned back to the fire, the thick lift of dark brown hair over his forehead, the somehow vulnerable shape of his neck above the dark-coloured shirt. That he should think himself incapable of fathering a child was the last thing that would have occurred to her. But now it was there like a tangible force in her brain, a force that clashed with the tender rays emanating from her heart.

How could she let Kyle, with his ardent wish—his need—for a son, think that the wish, the need, could never be realised? Pride of family, pride of name, was involved too ... how often had he held her and explained his deep need for a family, a son to take his place when the time came. 'Isn't it a fantastic thought, Jan, that our son will be the fourth generation to walk Masters land, to care for it and the people on it?'

But the cool eye of her brain saw only the man Kyle had become ... cold, cruel, heartless, a man who would have no qualms about claiming what was rightfully his, most of all the son he had dreamed of.

'Kyle,' she began carefully, wishing that she had curbed the spurt of retributory spirit that had caused that passionate encounter in front of Elena, 'if you and Elena—I mean, perhaps you would have—a son ...'

'Do you think I'd inflict myself on another woman knowing I'd be condemning her to childlessness?' he demanded roughly, his eyes reflecting to hers the blaze from the fire. Then the anger had seemed to leave him suddenly as he shrugged and looked away from her again. 'Go to bed, Jan, leave me alone.'

He returned to contemplation of his drink and seemed not to notice when Jan rose and left him a moment or two later. But when she looked back from the curving staircase he had dropped his head into his hands, a lonely figure who looked as if he had been dealt a mortal blow.

That thought had kept her awake until just before

dawn when she fell into a sleep of such deep oblivion
that she had not woken until Kyle shook her shoulder
roughly at eight to tell her the arrangements he had
made with Tom.

Now they were nearing the ranch and, as if sensing
this, Robbie's eyes pushed open and he smiled heart-
catchingly up into his mother's eyes before struggling
to an upright position on her lap. Secure with her arm
around him, he watched wide-eyed as Tom's hands
moved over the controls of the light plane as he
brought it down to land on the strip not far from the
house but hidden from it by the belt of trees enclosing
the working area. Which was why she hadn't noticed it
or the steel-spanned hangar where the plane was
housed.

'Fine boy you've got there, Jan,' Tom remarked
enigmatically before leaving his side of the plane to
come round and help her to the ground, continuing as
if his remarks had been uninterrupted: 'Spitting
image of his dad.'

Fear clutched Jan's chest and seemed to squeeze with
icy fingers. If it was so obvious to Tom that Kyle was
Robbie's father, wouldn't it be even more apparent to
Kyle himself? Tom's face was inscrutable as he leaned
inside to extract the luggage from the plane. He had
known Paul fairly well—wasn't it possible he was telling her that Robbie was like him?

Apprehension deepened in her when Tom pulled up
in front of the house in the covered jeep and took
Robbie, warmly enclosed in a brown hooded snowsuit,
while she disentangled the slender length of her legs
from the awkward vehicle.

'Will Kyle be back yet, Tom?' she asked, unable to
hide her nervousness as she received Robbie into her
arms again.

'Maybe—maybe not,' he grunted noncommittally as
he lifted the heavy suitcase from the back seat, setting
it down on the ground before reaching back in for the
high chair Jan had thought would be necessary. She

would have liked to bring Robbie's crib bed too, but that hadn't been possible. However, he could share the big bed with her in the master suite ... that way, neither of them would succumb to loneliness. A loneliness Robbie was bound to feel acutely after the boisterous company of Hilda's children.

Not that there had been much company for him that morning. Anna had been at school, Johann at work, and Hilda at the hospital beside Pieter, so that only the motherly neighbour woman from next door had been in the house with Robbie. A Robbie strangely subdued, as if he sensed the atmosphere of tension, and perhaps that was why his welcome for his mother was more enthusiastic than it might have been.

'Kyle mentioned he wanted to take a look at the creek up there where they're logging—making sure they leave enough trees for shade along the banks. Fish wouldn't last long if the whole thing was bared.'

Jan spared a quick glance at Tom's deeply lined face. It was from him that Kyle had absorbed most of his love for the land and everything on it, and Jan wondered how much persuasion Tom had needed to look with a less jaundiced eye on the lumber men whose saws must cut as deeply into his soul as into the creamy centres of the trees he loved. Quite a lot, it seemed, from his next words as they moved slowly in the direction of the house.

'I couldn't see why Kyle wanted to let them in. We were doing pretty well with the cattle, but'—he sighed—'he's a lot younger than me and sees things in a different way. And I have to admit there's sense in opening up some of the forest land for more grazing.'

Jan was only half listening, her thoughts leaping ahead to the house. Would Kyle be there? Unconsciously, her arms tightened round Robbie, an act he immediately rebelled against by squirming and pointing to the steps ahead.

'Walk, Mommy. Robbie walk,' he demanded, but Jan contained him until they had passed through the thick wood of the front door into the hall, which was already growing dim in the fading light.

'Guess Kyle isn't back yet.' Tom's voice sounded loud behind her as he dropped the luggage inside the door. 'Could be he dropped into the Pearson place on the way back, he often does.'

'Does he?'

Jan found it difficult to meet Tom's eyes and he showed unaccustomed embarrassment in his tone when he went on hurriedly to explain.

'Just to help out where he can. Now there's only Elena and her mother to run things, they need a man's help now and then.'

'Mr Pearson died?'

'About a year ago, and naturally Kyle has to be neighbourly.' His grey eyes took on an unmistakable shade of meaning when he added: 'I'm more glad than I can say that you're back—the young fellow too.' He smiled at Robbie's fearless investigation of his new surroundings.

'Tom,' Jan turned to him impulsively, 'Robbie is——'

'I know, honey.' Tom patted her arm in a fatherly way. 'You and Kyle will work things out in your own way. All it takes is a little time.'

He knew? What did he know? That Robbie was Kyle's child, or had Kyle told him that Paul——? A crash from the fireplace sent her scurrying across to right the stand of fire tools which Robbie's investigating fingers had knocked over. Scooping him up into her arms again, she scolded him gently.

'He has to find his bearings in his own way, too, Jan,' Tom put in as he came towards them with the high chair tucked under one brawny arm. 'Though I'd guess he needs a firm hand at times from the looks of him. You'll want this in the kitchen?'

'Please, Tom.'

Jan, close behind him, bumped against his back

when he halted abruptly after swinging open the kitchen door.

'Well, I'll be . . .' he exclaimed softly.

'What is it, Tom? What's wrong?' Jan lifted on to her toes to peer over his shoulder.

'I guess he did get back at that.'

Tom stepped aside and her eyes saw what his had been drawn to. On top of the stove a huge stew pot simmered gently, sending out a mouthwatering aroma of beef and mixed vegetables. Plates were warming in the glass-fronted oven below, and the table had been set with three places.

Sudden tears stung Jan's eyes. It was as if this homecoming was a normal one such as any loving family would experience after a time apart. But it wasn't . . . Hurt surged through her as she looked again round the kitchen with misty eyes. Kyle had probably realised that Tom would come into the house on their return, and what better way of convincing the older man that Kyle was doing his best to make the 'reconciliation' work? When he eventually let Jan go, the failure would be attributed to her and so save the pride Kyle prized so highly.

She set Robbie on the floor and remained bent over his small figure while she unzipped the snowsuit and slid it from him. Tom cleared his throat and stepped across the kitchen to place the chair next to the table.

'He's a good boy, Jan,' he said gruffly as he came past them again. Was he speaking about Robbie?—or Kyle? 'I'll take your suitcase upstairs for you, then I'll go see where Kyle is. Strange he didn't hear the plane come in if he's around.'

Was it so strange? Jan wondered as she went to hang Robbie's suit in the boot room near the back door, slipping off her own jacket and leaning her bent head against it after hanging it up. Kyle must hate the thought of another man's son, as he believed Robbie to be, taking the place in his home of the child he was convinced he would never have himself. Was he even now steeling himself to come into the house and see the living reminder of what he thought of as his own failure? How could she carry such a deception off, knowing what each day could do to Kyle? And she cared about the bitterness that would eat into his heart slowly like a poison, clouding his outlook so that he would never contemplate taking another wife.

'Mommy? Mommy!'

The beginnings of panic were in Robbie's questing words and Jan drew a deep shuddering breath to control her voice as she called: 'I'm here, darling. Let's go and see the place where we'll sleep.'

He made no objection to being swept up into her arms this time, and his arm went round her neck to clamp tightly there as they went towards the stairs, meeting Tom coming down.

'Everything's ready for you up there, young feller,' he said, one roughened finger reaching out to chuck Robbie under the chin. 'I'll have a look round for Kyle, Jan, but don't worry if he doesn't come home for a while. He must have been called out somewhere or he'd have been at the plane to meet you.'

'Thanks, Tom,' Jan smiled gratefully at his rangy figure which seemed out of place in these elegant surroundings. 'Will you come back and eat with us?'

'Not tonight, Jan,' he called back over his shoulder as he strode to the front door. 'Some other time maybe.'

Jan knew he was thinking of Kyle's obvious plan for a cosy family type meal for just the three of them and felt a moment of panic, wanting the support of Tom's placid kindliness when Kyle eventually came home.

'There's plenty——' she began, but the door had already closed with a dull thud behind him.

'Up there, Mommy?' Robbie pointed to the fascinating sweep of rails surrounding the upper galleried floor, and she continued up the stairs and across the spacious hall to the master bedroom.

'This is where you'll sleep, darling, with Mommy,' she told him, walking into the middle of the room and stopping with a gasp as her eyes fell on the open door into the dressing room.

Transformed since that morning, a cream-coloured high-sided crib bed occupied the narrow windowless wall, while a many-drawered dresser occupied the space under the wide, small-paned windows. When Robbie struggled to get down and explore this new and cosy set-up, Jan let him go with automatic hands, her mind numbed to everything but the chaotic thoughts churning through it. Where had the child's furniture come from? Kyle couldn't have known that Tom would come up here with the luggage—or could he? Had he left the dressing room door wide open with just that thought in mind? 'Look, Tom,' he could be saying, 'how I've done everything possible to make them comfortable and at home—if things go wrong, I can't be blamed.'

'Robbie's bed?' Already one small foot was wedged on the mattress between the spaced bars on the bed, and Jan said dully: 'Not with your shoes on, Robbie,' while her eyes took in the piled sheets and blankets on a rocking chair at one side of the crib. Had Tom noticed those too? she wondered with hurt waspishness. 'Let's go downstairs and get ready for supper, darling.'

She washed his hands and face and combed the thick darkness of his hair in the bathroom, touching up her make-up before descending again to where the stew still simmered appetisingly on the stove.

Robbie demanded his supper immediately, but Jan hastily scraped a stalk of celery and handed it to him in his high chair before turning back to the stove. A sampling taste told her that seasoning was needed, and she was adding salt with a shaker when the back door was suddenly thrust open and Kyle was there, bringing with him the crisp bite of the outdoors. Hatless, his hair seemed to crackle with vitality as it defied the careful brushing of some time ago, his cheeks holding a faint tinge of redness under the overlay of tan. His eyes met and locked with Jan's before moving to where Robbie stared wide-eyed at the sudden appearance of a stranger.

Jan's eyes were fixed on Kyle's face as he looked across the room at his son. The three of them seemed caught up in some sort of suspended animation as a series of expressions crossed Kyle's stilled features. Wariness gave way to surprise, surprise to deep-seated longing, and finally question as his eyes came slowly back to Jan. He knows, she thought with deadened awareness. He knows that Robbie is his son, and now he'll take him from me . . .

'He's a—fine boy,' he said in a cracked voice, unbuttoning his brown suede jacket as he moved quietly towards Robbie.

'Daddy?'

The childish word hung in the air with devastating clarity and Jan froze. Kyle's footsteps halted abruptly, and Robbie threw Jan an uncertain look. She closed her eyes and swallowed hard. Why hadn't she remembered that Robbie called any man coming home 'Daddy'? She knew that she should say something to break that pregnant hush, but her throat muscles refused to move. Then Kyle's feet were in motion again across the floor and he was talking to Robbie in a voice pitched to confidence-raising quietness.

The words he used were lost to Jan in the thunder of her heartbeat, but she saw Robbie smile suddenly into the man's face bent not too close to his. The sweet smile of confident friendliness which Robbie reserved for the special people of his life.

Pointing with a chubby finger, he told Kyle: 'That's Mommy.'

'Yes, I know. She's a pretty Mommy, isn't she?'

'Pretty Mommy,' Robbie agreed happily, throwing Jan a mischievous smile as if he knew what the words meant. His brown eyes watched as Kyle left to walk over to Jan.

'As I said, he's a fine boy,' he halted to say tautly, shrugging off his jacket to reveal a thick shirt of blue plaid.

'Th-thank you for all you've done,' Jan stammered, colour coming and going in her cheeks. 'Preparing supper, the bed for Robbie ...' Even if it was done for Tom's benefit, she added silently.

'I didn't think you'd feel like turning around and starting a meal from scratch when you got back,' he said noncommittally, going in the direction of the boot room and reappearing a moment later without his jacket. 'The crib is one that's been up in the attic since I got too old to use it.'

Ironic that his own son should now be the one to occupy the bed which had no doubt been saved for that purpose, although Kyle believed Robbie to be another man's child. That he did believe that was evident in the dead look about his eyes, the tightened line of his mouth as if containing a misery too great to be voiced.

'It—it was good of you to go to all that trouble. Robbie could have slept with me.'

A frown descended immediately between his brows. 'I wouldn't have thought that was a good habit to get into. One day he might resent giving up his place to another male.'

Jan turned back to the stove to hide the painful rush of colour to her neck and face. 'That's a problem he won't have to worry about.'

'No?' The word hung in the air between them as Jan stirred the stew mindlessly. 'What about Don McLeish? Won't he expect sole rights in your bed when you divorce me and marry him?'

Dropping the spoon she had been stirring with, Jan whirled to face the mocking smile twisting his lips. 'What he or any other man expects doesn't concern me in the least. Robbie's the only person I care about.'

'That could cause a bundle of misery when he wants to branch out, maybe marry——'

'Something like the misery your grandmother caused when you married me?' she flashed, looking abstractedly over at Robbie when he renewed his pleas for supper. 'I have to feed Robbie soon,' she said with averted head.

'I'll be down in ten minutes.' His voice had a hard edge to it, but it softened noticeably when he paused to speak lightly to Robbie on his way to the door. A moment later Jan heard the chink of bottle on glass as he poured himself a drink in the living room.

In a remarkably short time he was back, his hair flattened damply from the shower, his chin less blue after the application of a razor, though the white high-necked sweater he wore threw his whole head into dark relief.

Jan had already started Robbie on his meal, and he looked with partially sated eyes when Kyle took the chair opposite and grinned at him.

'Robbie hungry,' he explained guilelessly as Jan spooned another mouthful of gravy-rich stew into his willingly parted lips.

'Kyle's hungry too.' He gave Jan a sideways glance. 'Why don't you let me feed Robbie while you organise ours?'

'Robbie can feed himself,' she returned shortly, letting the spoon go into her son's chubby fingers.

'They why are you doing it for him?' The question was asked with inoffensive blandness, but Jan flushed angrily.

'Because—because he's in a strange place, and I want him to know that I'm here.'

'But he can see you're here,' he put in with irrefutable logic, then his voice softened somewhat. 'He'll only feel strange if you give him the impression that he should feel that way. He seems the kind of boy who doesn't care where he is as long as you're within sight and sound.'

Resentment bubbled up in Jan and she rose abruptly to serve their dinner from the pot. No one else had ever questioned her handling of her son ... there had been nothing but admiration for her hard battle to support him without benefit of a husband. Yet here was Kyle telling her twice within the last half hour that she was being a dominating mother, the kind of woman who tied her son to her apron strings.

'Don't look so mad,' he warned quietly when she placed his plate before him with little grace then went to sit close to Robbie. 'That's one sure way to upset him.'

Jan made no reply, and the meal was eaten in silence apart from Robbie's often unintelligible chatter to which he seemed not to need an answer. But when Jan rose to clear away the dishes, Kyle spoke.

'I'm sorry I wasn't here to meet you at the plane. I'd intended to be there, but I had a call from the Pearson place. An emergency, Elena said, though it turned out to be nothing like that.'

The whimsical smile about his lips flicked a raw nerve in Jan and she turned away too quickly, the top plate of the three in her hand sliding off and falling to the floor with a crash of broken china. Inexplicable tears formed in her eyes as she gazed helplessly down at the shattered plate, tears she was unable to hide from Kyle when he took the other dishes from her hands and set them on the counter before turning back to put firm hands on her shoulders.

'I'm sorry,' she choked, fighting an almost irresistible impulse to lay her head against his shoulder and have those hands hold her with the fierce yet gentle touch she remembered so well.

'Jan, if there's one thing we have a surfeit of, it's plates. They're stacked in the cupboards, in the attics, in the cellar.' He shook her without force, and for a wild moment she sensed that he was drawing her to him in a motion of comfort, but then he said quietly: 'You're tired, it's been quite a day for you. The fire's alight, so why don't you take Robbie into the living room while I make us some coffee? And here,' he felt in his pocket and took out an unused white handkerchief, 'wipe your eyes. Don't let him see you cry.'

He half lifted the linen square to her face as if intending to wipe away the offending tears himself, then he thrust it abruptly into her hand and bent swiftly to pick up the pieces at their feet. Listlessly Jan dabbed at her eyes, thankful that Robbie's attention was distracted momentarily by the small notebook Kyle must have taken from his pocket and handed to him before coming to her side.

What Kyle had said was true ... she was tired. Tired already of the deception she would have to carry on as long as she stayed at Silvercreek. If only he had remained cool and withdrawn—or even blazing with the hatred he felt for her—it would have been easier to deceive him. It was his gentleness she couldn't take, that glimpse into the tender-hearted Kyle she had once loved, even though it was for Robbie's sake that he had spoken quietly, kindly.

She lifted the boy from his chair, leaving Kyle's notebook on the table before leaving the kitchen and going upstairs with Robbie on her arm to open the suitcase and take from it his honey-coloured stuffed toy squirrel and picture books. They were sitting side by side on the wide sofa when Kyle came into the room bearing a tray with three mugs ... brown earthenware mugs. Jan glanced swiftly up at his darkly chiselled face, but found no trace of remembrance in the deep-set eyes and firmly held mouth.

'Hot chocolate for Robbie—is that okay?' he asked without looking at her.

'Y-yes, fine.'

She took her own mug from the tray he held out to her, and put Robbie's on the side table beside her until it cooled. Kyle left his on the tray, setting it down on the table beside the armchair he settled into, his eyes brushing over Jan and meeting Robbie's.

'Who's that you've got there?'

Robbie held the squirrel up and looked into the surprisingly realistic face. 'That's Bobo.'

'Bobo? That's a funny name for a squirrel—why don't you bring him over and let me see him?'

Robbie needed no second bidding, and before Jan could stop him he had slid from the thick cushions and was leaning against Kyle's long leg, holding the childish toy up for his close inspection. The big brown man's hand curled round it, dwarfing the furred figure.

'Hi, Bobo,' he said softly, and Jan's heart contracted when the other hand came down to lift Robbie and set him down on one knee, the short legs dangling between powerfully muscled thighs. Robbie cast not one look in Jan's direction, seeming fascinated as his eyes hung on the man's face above his, watching the movement of Kyle's lips and glimpsing the strong even teeth behind them while he talked with apparent seriousness to the inanimate squirrel.

A shiver ran over Jan and she averted her eyes from them when Robbie crowed delightedly, his tiny pearly-toothed smile reaching up to meet Kyle's. Lifting her coffee mug, she swallowed convulsively of the warm liquid and got up restlessly to sit at one side of the broad hearth, cup in hand, eyes directed sightlessly into the flames leaping beside her.

No, it wasn't possible for her to stay on here, to see a relationship develop between the two people who meant more to her than life itself. She would give up her life gladly ... but she couldn't give up Robbie. And that's what she would have to do if Kyle discovered that her son was his, too. The hate he felt for her, for the woman he was convinced she was, would never allow any compromise.

'It's time for bed, Robbie,' she said, her voice harshly coloured from her thoughts as she rose and set her mug on the tray beside Kyle's chair.

'He hasn't drunk his chocolate yet,' Kyle reminded

her, his eyes faintly puzzled as they studied her agitated face. 'He'll be okay with me if you want to get things ready up there.' Robbie squirmed off his knee to run to the sofa and the books he had left there. 'Or don't you trust me with him?'

'Of course I trust you. It's just that he—he's tired, it's past his bedtime already.'

'Don't you think it might be better if he's a little more tired than usual tonight?' he suggested, his forehead grooved as he looked up at Jan. 'A strange house, a strange bed ...'

'Yes, I suppose so,' she agreed helplessly, knowing he was right. 'But he might fuss when I go upstairs.'

That likelihood was far from apparent as Robbie came back loaded with books and accepted with royal unconcern his reinstatement on Kyle's knee.

'Mommy won't be long, Robbie,' Jan said with a faint air of desperation and flushed when Robbie gave her an absent smile.

'Mommy long,' he repeated, and spread open the most colourful page of his favourite book for Kyle's inspection.

Catching her breath against the hurt surging through her, Jan turned quickly and made for the stairs, resentment tightening her lips and bringing a flinty spark to her eyes. It was as if Kyle had deliberately set out to prove how unnecessary she was in Robbie's life, how little he would miss her if ... But she wouldn't let him do it, she told herself fiercely as she reached the top of the stairs and looked down to where Robbie was docilely drinking the chocolate milk with Kyle's help. She wouldn't let him dismiss all the heartache, all the struggle she had had to keep Robbie with her. She would fight for her son and ...

Her hand went up to hold her head as she sank on to the bed and leaned against the curved wood post at its end. Of course that wasn't so. Kyle had no idea of the truth of Robbie's birth, no thought of luring his affections away from her. His offer to stay with the boy had been no more than an extension of the kindness he had shown earlier.

But the ease of Robbie's capitulation still left a lingering hurt.

CHAPTER SEVEN

ROBBIE was asleep on Kyle's chest when Jan came down the stairs once more, his hair deepened to blackness in contrast with the white sweater. For a moment while she hesitated at the foot of the stairs she thought Kyle slept too, but his head lifted and turned from the fire when she crossed the floor.

'Sorry, he went to sleep so fast I couldn't do anything about it,' he said softly, a bemusedly contented look about his face. 'Everything ready?'

Jan nodded, aches she didn't want to feel spreading from her heart to form a lump in her throat.

'I'll carry him up for you.' Using one arm to hold the unconscious Robbie, Kyle rose without effort and followed Jan up the carpeted stairs to the master bedroom. Seeing the pyjamas she had laid out on the bed, he gently lowered Robbie to the white spread and stood back. To Jan's surprise, he made no move to leave the room but stood and watched while she fumbled with the fastenings on Robbie's clothes.

'Aren't you going to take his shoes off first?' he asked drily, keeping his voice to a low pitch.

Jan gazed stupidly down at the brown leather tied shoes, knowing there had been a reason somewhere in her subconscious for not removing those shoes first as she always did. She had already slid them from the small feet when it hit her. Robbie's toes! The little ones with their distinctive inward and downward curve. An outsider would scarcely notice such a minor aberration, but Kyle, who had often laughed with her about the 'Masters' curse' would be drawn to it immediately. And know . . .

Jan cast a half fearful, half irritated look over her shoulder and Kyle said: 'Does it bother you that I'm here?'

'Yes ... a little,' she admitted shortly, and turned back to the sleeping child.

'I'd hoped——' Kyle began, and stopped. 'Will you come down when he's settled? I'd like to talk to you, Jan.'

'I'm very tired, Kyle. Won't it wait till tomorrow?'

'No.' The one word was final, decisive as he turned to the door. 'I'll be waiting.'

The hint of steel under the flatly spoken words left no room for refusal, and Jan's fingers trembled as she pulled on Robbie's pyjamas, tucking his feet into the detachable toed part of the sleepers with a sigh of thankfulness that most of his pyjamas were similarly equipped. But was her relief premature? Did Kyle know, and had he kept the knowledge within himself until Robbie could no longer be upset by raised voices, angry words?

But when she went downstairs, after spending longer than usual beside the crib looking down at the deeply sleeping child, Kyle rose calmly enough from his chair and asked what she would like to drink.

'I'll get some coffee,' she said jerkily, escaping to the kitchen where she stared round at the immaculate counter tops and scoured sink. Her eyes went to the floor and found it washed clean where gravy from the shattered plate had marked the gold vinyl. She jumped when Kyle spoke behind her.

'I think I'll have coffee too. Why don't we just take the pot into the living room? It should keep warm beside the fire.'

But even when she was settled in the armchair opposite his, like the contentedly happy married couple they might have aspired to being once, Jan found it hard to meet the almost speculative look he sent across the hearth to her. There was something about him tonight—a stillness, a quietness as if his thoughts had gone deep and found some measure of peace within himself. Whatever she was bracing herself to hear him say, the words he used were the last she expected.

'Are you in love with McLeish, Jan?'

Her eyes widened and locked with the steady regard of his, seeing the intentness in the brown eyes that waited for her answer. Unable to think clearly, she dropped hers to the brown liquid in the earthenware mug clasped in her hands. One glimpse had been enough to prove that his reason for asking the question was far from being prompted by a rekindling of his love for her.

'What can that possibly mean to you?' she asked in a voice made harsh with hurt.

Kyle put down his cup on the hearth and leaned forward, an elbow on each knee, and said quietly: 'It could mean a lot if you're thinking of marrying him just to make a home for your son, to give him a father.'

Jan's breath drew in sharply, but her indignation was tempered by the honest appraisal of her feelings and the immediate conclusion that if she married Don it would be for that reason—to provide Robbie with a normal family life, a male figure to identify with. But she snapped contrarily:

'Aren't you forgetting that other need I have? That insatiable need for——'

'I was wrong about that,' his voice, though subdued, overrode hers as he stood up and looked down into her face. 'And I'm sorry. I didn't know about the child —or Paul's death.' He turned to face the glowing logs, one hand going to rub the back of his neck as if to ease tension there.

'I did a lot of thinking last night,' he went on, 'and—well, I think I can see more clearly what went wrong with—us.' He turned and paced away from the fire area, back to the more open space behind the sofa. 'We married too soon ... you were so young, and after the kind of life you'd had, you would have married any man who offered security and a home, a name. I happened to be the first one to come along to fulfil those needs.'

Disbelief rounded Jan's eyes and opened her lips as he spoke. It was as if the love between them had never been. Kyle saw himself as a man used for the material assets he could provide for the poor young orphan girl who had spent all her early life waiting to fall into the arms of the first man to make the offer of security. She sprang to her feet, her cheeks flaming.

'I had no need of your *charity*!' she scorned. 'I had a good job, my own little apartment ...' She stopped and drew a trembling breath when he shook his head calmly.

'Those weren't the things you wanted—still want, Jan. It was a home you craved, a family ...' His jaw clamped down on the last word as if it pained him to say it, then his lips moved again stiffly. 'You have a child now, and I'm offering you the home you'd be marrying Don McLeish for.'

Jan's hands curled slowly into fists at her sides, the colour drained from her face as she stared into the deepset brown of his eyes across the sofa back. The blankness in his expression reflected nothing of tenderness, of caring, or ... love. There was even less feeling there than if he had been making a deal with a buyer of his cattle.

'That's not possible.' She turned away and stared into the fire, trying unsuccessfully to still the trembling of her legs.

'Does that mean you *are* in love with McLeish?'

Kyle was beside her suddenly, his fingers bruising the soft flesh of her upper arm as he turned her forcefully to face him. As if he was under tremendous strain, the skin over his cheekbones was stretched to gaunt tautness.

Despair washed over Jan as she looked up into the familiar eyes, recognising abstractedly the light yellow flecks mingled with the brown. 'I'm not in love with anyone,' she denied shakily. 'The only love that ever meant anything to me is dead.'

The lines beside Kyle's mouth deepened as his lips grew tight and bloodless. His hand dropped away from her arm and he half turned away from her. 'Paul,' he muttered almost inaudibly.

'Paul?'

'It's only natural you should feel that way about the father of your child.'

Hysteria bubbled up inside Jan, a wildness brought on by tiredness and the emotional strains of the day. 'My child's father—yes, I'll always love him. No other man could ever mean more than a particle of what I feel for him.'

Suddenly Kyle was shaking her, his hard fingers bruising the softness of her flesh under the off-white top of her pants suit. 'But Paul's dead, Jan! You can't spend the rest of your life in limbo because of a tragic accident that took him from you. You're the kind of woman who needs a man, a husband——'

'Oh, we're back to that again, are we?' Jan stepped away from his hands and sat in the armchair again, looking up at him with a mocking smile. 'Were you planning on supplying that need too?'

Kyle's eyes went over her face and hair and dropped to touch lightly on the rounded curves of her figure. 'Not necessarily,' he said tersely, turning away to stride over to the bar, evidently forgetting his earlier resolve to drink coffee.

Jan heard the chink of bottle on glass and then he was back, handing her the same measure of brandy as she had swallowed the first night of her return.

'That isn't the important thing,' he went on as if the conversation had never been interrupted. 'Robbie's the one who matters in this. Paul was my friend, and I'd like to be the one to bring up his son—as my own.'

'You mean——?' she gazed up at him incredulously, her eyes seeming to cling to his.

'I mean that as far as anyone else is concerned, he *is* my son. He would bear my name, have a good home and education, and one day inherit the ranch. Paul and I were enough alike physically so that Robbie could pass easily as mine. In fact, when I saw him to-day, I thought . . .' His words were clamped off abruptly and it was a full minute before he went on in more controlled tones: 'So there would be no doubts in anyone's mind. He could have a happy, secure life——'

'With parents who hate each other?' she interjected bitterly, and saw his expression harden. She gulped blindly at the brandy, willing herself not to choke as its fumes rose dizzily to her head and spread molten warmth down the length of her body.

'It doesn't have to be that way,' Kyle returned shortly, moving away from her to take the chair oppo-site, his elbows on his knees again, but this time his hands caressed the brandy glass. Jan seemed unable to move her eyes from his long lean fingers which were almost the same shade of dark brown as the liquid they circled. The nails were cut short, masculine in the same way as were the dark hairs emerging from his wrists below the cuffs of his white sweater. His chest, too, was covered with the same dark springy hair, she remembered . . . She shook her head slightly and looked with dazed eyes into Kyle's face when he spoke again.

'I'm not saying it would be smooth going to begin with,' he said soberly, 'but in time—well, we could work out some kind of a relationship that would be satisfactory to both of us.'

Satisfactory! Jan leaned back in her chair and closed her eyes against the penetrating look he had levelled at her. Could any relationship between herself and Kyle be considered satisfactory if it excluded the warmth of love, the heat of passion they had once stirred in each other? A too clearly etched vision of future coolly polite encounters sent a shiver over Jan's frame and she stood up, her shoulders drooping in unconscious defeat.

'It wouldn't work,' she said dully. 'How long do you think we could fool other people into believing we're a normal married couple? Your friends, the ranch people ...'

He rose smoothly to stand before her, but he refrained from touching her this time, though his voice had deepened with an emotion she couldn't even guess at.

'The other day, up there'—his head inclined backward to the upper floor—'proved how normal a marriage it could be.'

'No!'

'Why not, Jan?'

Now he gripped her arms, shaking her slightly but with a quality of gentleness that made her raise her eyes to his face. The colour had leached out beneath the weathered tan of his skin and his eyes burned with dark intensity as they blazed into hers. 'Okay, so you fell for Paul ... it's not exactly unknown for a wife— or a husband, for that matter—to realise they've made a mistake. But before that ... before you and Paul met, we seemed to be suited well enough. In time, maybe we can——'

'No—no!' Jan twisted from his grasp and put up her hands to cover her face, her fingers trembling visibly. 'Without love ...'

'We could learn to be happy again together,' he urged persistently, his voice matching the paleness of his face. 'Paul's dead, Jan, and ... you're still a woman with normal needs, just as I'm a man with those same——'

'How can you talk that way?' she choked, taking her hands away from her face and looking at him with mingled scorn and horror. 'As if it's all just a—an act of physical release! It has to be more than that ... for me, at least.'

'All right, forget that part of it,' he said bleakly. 'Let's just stick to the basic facts that you need a settled home and I—I need a son.'

'That's what you've always wanted, isn't it?' she said with slow awareness, her eyes darkened emotionally. 'A son to carry on the Masters line. It didn't really matter to you who the mother was as long as she'd warm your bed and provide what you wanted.' She gave a short, brittle laugh. 'And you suspected that Elena would be cold comfort on long winter nights, didn't you?'

'Stop it!' Kyle's nostrils flared whitely, and for a moment Jan felt a flicker of fear, a tremor that died when he turned away and thrust his hands into his pockets as if schooling himself not to hit her. 'This isn't getting us anywhere. Will you at least think about it?' he ended abruptly, his eyes revealing more than he would have cared to admit verbally. It was vitally important for him to have a son, even one he believed to have been fathered by another man.

'I'll think about it,' she agreed evenly, and made her way to the stairs, hardly noticing that they said no goodnights. She would think about it—oh, how she would think about it!—but she knew with each upward step she took that there could only be one answer.

It was only as Jan stood looking down at her sleeping son that a decision became complicated. All the time she had been undressing, slipping the translucent folds of a nylon nightdress over her head and washing in the adjoining bathroom, there had been an accompanying insistent beat of negative thought. The impossibility of agreeing to Kyle's suggestion was obvious in the heart-sinking feeling she had whenever she thought of remaining at Silvercreek as his wife, yet not his wife in the full sense of the word. Not for a moment would the ranch wives—women who cared deeply for their husbands or they would not remain with them in this isolated situation—be deceived by Jan's slight acting ability. It would be a double act, she told herself wryly as she rubbed cream savagely into her skin. Hiding from outsiders the fact that the 'reconciliation' was unreal, and from Kyle that she loved him, were far beyond that ability.

And that she still loved him was a fact she had striven against acknowledging during all the months, the years, of their separation. Hatred had been spread like a thin veneer over her true emotions ... volatile emotions which had needed only the touch of his mouth on hers, the feel of his hard body against the softness of hers to spring to life ... vibrant, devastating life.

Yet love was more than just the satisfaction of the senses. It was a mutual caring, a sharing of problems and joys of everyday living. The kind of love Kyle would merely pay lip service to in his eagerness for an heir to Silvercreek.

Robbie, when she went to check on him, slept soundly on his back, dark lashes carving half moons on baby round flushed cheeks. A tender smile touched Jan's lips as she pulled the blankets closer under his chin. He had settled down at Silvercreek as if he belonged here.

At the thought, her smile disappeared to be replaced by a faint frown between her eyes. Robbie did belong here, in the land of his father and forefathers. Here he would grow tall and lean and strong like his father, learning to love the land as Kyle did and, when the time came, taking his place with the pride that could only come from the secure knowledge of his heritage. Had she the right to deny him that birthright, knowing the alternatives open to her? Marriage to Don, a man she was deeply fond of but could never love in entirety, and a city upbringing which surely all Robbie's inherited traits would rebel against. A single life, her son being brought up in the too intensive care of his mother ... Kyle had been right in that, at least. She was honest enough to admit to herself that without a strong male hand in his life, Robbie could well turn out to be self-centred and mother-oriented.

Long hours of tossing in the wide master bed brought no clearcut decision, and it was close to dawn when she fell into a deep and dreamless sleep. She had heard Kyle come upstairs just after two as if he, too, had had restless thoughts too disturbing to permit rest.

It was late when Robbie's insistent calling penetrated the drugged mists of sleep. Forcing reluctant lids open, Jan glanced at the bedside clock and saw with an immediate sigh of relief that the hands pointed to just after eight. Kyle would have gone by now, and she would have the whole day to think, to make the decision which would affect her son's life more than any she would ever make for him.

But her relief was shortlived. She was in the kitchen preparing a soft-boiled egg for Robbie while he spooned cereal hungrily into his mouth when the back door opened, bringing in an icy gust of air. Before she could turn from the stove, Robbie's delighted 'Daddy!' told her it was Kyle who stood there after closing the door quickly behind him.

Her eyes met his, and she looked away in embarrassment at the look she saw there. Jerkily, she explained: 'He calls every man that—even Don.' She sensed rather than saw Kyle's measured nod as he slid off his brown suede jacket and hung it in the boot room.

'Well, I don't know what it does for Don,' he remarked casually when he emerged and went past her with his easy stride, 'but it makes me feel a hundred feet tall.' He looked back into her stricken eyes and asked: 'Any chance of some coffee?'

'It's nearly ready, I'll bring it.'

'Well, Robbie, how'd you like to come and see a real Bobo after breakfast?' Kyle ruffled the boy's neatly brushed hair before taking the chair opposite.

'Bobo?' Robbie's eyes were round with puzzlement, staring across as if overwhelmed by Kyle's broad-shouldered masculinity.

'Are there still squirrels around?' Jan was startled into asking when she took away Robbie's cereal plate and replaced it with a smaller dish of chopped buttered egg and finger pieces of toast.

'There's a couple still getting ready for the snow in that belt of trees beyond the corrals,' Kyle explained, looking up at her with sober eyes that reflected thoughts far removed from squirrels.

Jan shifted her gaze to Robbie's untouched plate. 'Eat your egg, Robbie,' she instructed sharply, and turned away to pour two mugs of coffee. Breakfast seemed suddenly unappetising to her, but she longed for the hot fragrance of freshly brewed coffee.

'Thanks,' Kyle murmured as she set his mug before him and rolled up the sleeves of his denim shirt to his elbows before lifting it to his mouth. Jan averted her eyes from the sinewy display of taut muscles partially disguised by the dark fuzz of hair covering them, but she was conscious of his penetrating gaze which she knew took in the smudges of darkness under her eyes, the pallor of her skin without make-up.

'You didn't sleep much,' he said quietly. 'Does that mean you've come to a decision?'

Jan glanced at Robbie and saw that he was absorbed by his egg and toast, his head bent and a frown of concentration between his eyes. The same frown that had reminded her so often of Kyle. If she decided to stay, how long would it be before Kyle himself saw that likeness, even if by some miracle she could keep from him the telltale formation of his son's toes? And could she live with such lies if that were possible? But she had been through all those tortuous thoughts last night without coming to a solution.

'Jan?'

She drew in her breath and said shakily: 'Kyle, I——' The words of confession froze in her throat and she felt the firm grip of his fingers on her arm.

'Just say you'll try it for a while,' he urged. 'You were going to stay anyway until the team comes back next month, and you need somewhere to stay till the trouble's over in Vancouver at the place where you were living.' His voice hardened. 'I've no intention of asking any more of you than you're willing to give.'

Pale rose coloured Jan's cheeks and she lowered her eyes to the table. If only he knew how much she was willing to give ... if he loved her. But he didn't. Bitterness had run too deep for that. If he found out that Robbie was his son, he wouldn't hesitate to throw out the woman he was convinced had only cared for him because of the material things he could provide.

Against that, there was Robbie's inalienable right to take his place here as a Masters. Was it possible that, given time, she and Kyle could recapture the love they had lost? And that she could then tell him the truth of Robbie's birth without fear of being parted from her child?

'All right, Kyle,' she nodded her agreement, turning her eyes away from the sudden lightening in his. A son was so very important to him!

'See Bobo?' Robbie queried, looking first at his mother and then at Kyle.

'Daddy will take you just as soon as Mommy can get you dressed,' Kyle promised, a new emotional depth to his voice as his eyes went from the shining eagerness of Robbie's to the shadowed violet of Jan's. 'You won't regret it, Jan, I promise you,' he said steadily.

She shook her head and lifted the demanding Robbie from the chair. She was committed now, but who was to say whether or not she would regret it? Certainly not Kyle, with his ignorance of the truth on almost all counts.

Days passed, blending into one another with an ease that denied the doubts which assailed Jan only when she lay alone in the big bed, the house silent around her. Silent but for the occasional sleepy murmur from Robbie through the open door between their rooms, and now and then a restless creak as Kyle turned over in the room opposite.

Together under one roof ... yet apart in separate worlds of their own. Kyle had relaxed visibly, the lines round his mouth and eyes lessening until they were only noticeable when he looked up at Jan after playing on the living room floor with Robbie, or when he brought him back from some foray into the ranch area.

Robbie himself seemed to have blossomed and grown older under the unknown circumstance of having a man, tall and strong, centre his attention on him alone. Adoration beamed from his round brown eyes whenever Kyle appeared, his very presence promising untold delights of new experiences in the shape of horses, cows, and the lesser animals necessary on a self-supporting ranch.

As for Jan, the days went by in mingled pain and happiness. Happiness in knowing how their lives might have been, pain in the ever-growing certainty that Kyle's need was for his son, not the wife he believed had never really loved him. But how long could she hide from him the joy that set her heart hammering when he pushed open the kitchen door, Robbie in his brown snowsuit perched easily on one arm, two pairs of identical brown eyes reaching for her as if in reassurance that she was there preparing the meal they would all enjoy together? Or the electric tensing of her body when Kyle's hand brushed hers accidentally?

Only in this bed, where they had loved so passionately, did she give free rein to the imagination that saw Kyle take her into his arms, his voice husky with need for her, the years between wiped out as if they had never been. It was the same imagination that kept her tossing and turning till the early hours of each morning, so that her eyes developed permanent dark lines under their vivid dark blue irises, her cheeks thinned and grew paler, her figure lost some of its roundness.

Evenings, too, held the bitter-sweetness of what might have been. Often Jan thought wryly that anyone looking in on them would have thought them a typical ranch couple. Kyle, after a long day of physical

labour, would settle back in his chair beside the leaping fire, long legs stretched out before him, a book in
his hand, while Jan sat opposite mending Robbie's
clothes or reading herself, their child safely tucked up
in bed on the floor above.

But an onlooker would have heard no cosy murmurs
of intimacy between the man and woman sitting there.
Only politely restrained remarks with long pauses between. Sometimes, when Jan lifted her head to glance
across at the deceptively relaxed figure opposite, she
would catch Kyle's eyes on her, the same remote speculative look in their depths that she had noticed earlier.
There was never time for more than a glimpse, however, because he would immediately stand up and
excuse himself on the grounds that he had work to do
in the study.

Until one night five days after Robbie had been
brought to the ranch.

Jan had been staring absently into the fire, her book
neglected on her lap, and unconsciously let a sigh
escape her.

'Why don't you go and watch television?' Kyle asked
quietly over the top of the farm manual he was reading.

'Television?' she stammered, gathering up her scattered thoughts and frowning across at the matching
crease between his brows. 'I—I thought you must have
got rid of it.'

'You mean you haven't been into that room since
you came?' His head indicated the door of what Jan
would always consider his grandmother's room.

'No,' she returned quickly, glancing eloquently at
the white-painted door and away again.

'It's not the same now, Jan,' he told her after a
slight hesitation, his voice low and strained. 'It's been
completely——'

'No, I don't want to see it!' Jan's breath had begun
to come in quick gasps and she felt as if she would
suffocate. However the room had been changed, she

would still see the arrogant dark-skinned woman sitting in an armchair by the fire, her fierce black eyes looking contemptuously at the granddaughter-in-law she hadn't wanted. Pointing out in word and attitude how unsuitable she thought the bride Kyle had chosen for himself.

'I think you should,' Kyle insisted quietly, getting up and coming to stand over her chair. 'There are programmes it might be good for Robbie to see later on, and——' He broke off and brought himself down to a level with her eyes, seeming to trap their distressed blue in the yellow-flecked brown of his. 'Gran changed a lot before she died, Jan. She——'

'Bully for her! I hope her deathbed confessions cleared her conscience satisfactorily!'

'She realised she hadn't been—fair to you.'

'*Fair?*' Jan echoed bitterly. 'She didn't know the meaning of the word! Vindictiveness, yes. Arrogance, yes. She knew every shade of meaning for those words, but nothing about kindness ... love ...' To her horror, Jan felt her lower lip tremble uncontrollably, warm tears rushing to her eyes so that she turned her head away from his, which was too near for comfort.

Too gentle, also, were the arms that raised her from the chair with little effort, crossing behind her back as Kyle drew her body to the shelter of his. One hand was released and came up to raise her chin so that her brimming eyes, the irises like drenched violets, looked miserably into his.

'Jan ...'

His voice held the huskiness so familiar to her, the depth that had always been a prelude to the storm of emotion that would sweep them up and carry them off into a world of their own making ... the lean line of his body was tensed like a tightly coiled spring, white heat conveying itself from muscled chest, stomach and thighs to her own corresponding softness.

'Jan,' he said again, and his head bent until she felt the hurried warmth of his breath on her face. Her own breath seemed suspended, her tears stilled as her vision filled with his eyes, darkened almost to blackness, the slight disorder of his hair as it fell over his brow, the blue shadows along the tight line of his jaw.

Her lips parted to meet the descent of his hard warm mouth, her eyes closing as if to contain the wildfire jumping through her veins ... a forest fire that was running out of control in a way that frightened her and brought her hands up against his chest to push him away with a strength born of panic. What he felt for her was physical desire, not the rekindling of love born of a mutual need to share every facet of their lives. Her breath came out in a series of gasps.

'Don't, Kyle ... leave me alone ... I don't want ...'

He let her go with such suddenness that she staggered back and fell into the chair, her breast rising and falling rapidly under the thin blue wool of her tunic top as she struggled for control.

'Sorry,' he said briefly, coldly, and turned away to go to the bar, pouring whisky for himself and making a longer drink for her, thrusting it into her hand and retreating again to the other side of the fireplace. He took a long gulp of his drink before turning to regard her with sardonically raised brows.

'It's not exactly easy to live in the same house with someone as attractive as you without——'

'I'm not goods to be looked over and pawed at any man's whim!' she flared, recovering rapidly from the weakness brought about by the contact with his vital masculinity, which was evident even now in his aggressive stance before the fire. One brow lifted even higher as he looked down at her.

'It sounds as if Women's Lib has had its effect on you.'

'Certainly it has,' she snapped back at him, 'if that means I don't have to make myself available to any male who takes a fancy to my physical assets!'

'I'm not exactly any male, am I?' He stared thoughtfully into the depths of his glass. 'We were married once'—his head lifted and he looked at her, bright meaning in his eyes—'we still are, for that matter. Who could blame me for wanting our reconciliation to be complete in every way?'

'I could, for one,' she returned smartly, 'when it's based on nothing more than the—the physical.'

'That wasn't the way it was with you and Paul?'

Warily, she eyed him. One false word and he would know there had been nothing, not even the physical, between herself and Paul. And that would lead him to other conclusions ...

'I've changed my mind,' she said abruptly, standing and putting her untouched glass on the side table. 'I'd like to see your grandmother's room.'

For a long moment he stared at her, then gave a dismissing shrug and laid his own glass down before leading the way to the white-painted door close to the stairs.

Jan's heart began to beat like a trip-hammer as the door swung open under Kyle's hand, which then went to two switches inside the doorway. Her pulses quieted suddenly as she stepped over the threshold past him and gazed bemusedly round the room.

Nothing, absolutely nothing, remained to remind her of the autocratic old lady. No old-fashioned bed by a small-paned window, no well-used chair angled close to the fireplace. Instead, there was a burst of floral lightness from the gaily covered, deeply cushioned chairs and sofa arranged in such a way as to make a focal point of the large television screen to one side of the fireplace.

A fireplace no longer composed of weathered brick, but painted white in keeping with the general air of brightness. In place of the small window, which had allowed little light into the room, were wide and long sliding windows leading to a small illuminated patio edged with what would be flower borders in the summer.

'Oh ...' she breathed involuntarily, unaware of the

man's searching eyes on her face. 'It's ... beautiful!'

She looked round and up into his eyes then, wondering if he had remodelled this room with her in mind—he had told her it would be her sitting room one day when his grandmother no longer needed it. But there was only tightness in the lines round his mouth and eyes, nothing of remembrance.

'It makes a good family room,' he nodded, his eyes growing bleak as they went to the windows. 'Or so I thought when I planned it. The patio's fenced in so that the only damage kids could do would be to dig up the flower beds.'

Children he had hoped to have with Elena? Children he believed were now impossible for him. Pain constricted Jan's breathing, a choking ache that intensified as she looked up to the lines etched in bitterness round his mouth. Guilt brought sudden dryness to her lips and she licked nervously at them with the tip of her tongue. If she could persuade Kyle that children were possible for him, perhaps he would let her go and take Robbie with her. At that moment, being parted permanently from the man she loved was by far the lesser threat than the one posed by the possibility of having her son taken from her.

'Kyle, you could ...' Her voice faltered and died away as he brought the pointed sharpness of his eyes to bear on her.

'I could—what?'

'It's possible you could have children with Elena,' she said in a rush, turning her back to him and gazing sightlessly out to the artificially lit bare earth of the flower borders. 'I've heard—read—that with someone else——'

'That's a risk I'm not prepared to hang on any woman,' he returned harshly, and wheeled away to the door, turning there to look back expressionlessly at her. 'Is there anything you want to watch tonight?'

'No ... no, I think I'll go on to bed now. Robbie wakes early.'

He stood back to let her pass, then flicked off the two switches before closing the door and bypassing her to stride to the fireplace, picking up his glass from the table and returning to the bar.

'You haven't touched your drink,' he said shortly, glancing over his shoulder as she paused on the bottom stair.

'You forget that I never did care for liquor,' she said, her voice quiet but carrying. 'You used to be satisfied, too, with a lot less than you drink now.'

'I have to be satisfied with a lot less in many ways,' he drawled, crossing lazily to the foot of the stairs and looking up to where she now stood at the curve. 'Whisky is something I don't have to stint on. It's mine for the taking, unlike some of the other pleasures I'm forced to forgo these days.'

The insolent raking of his eyes over her curving figure left no doubt as to just which pleasure he referred to.

'Goodnight, Kyle.'

For a moment she wondered if he would follow her, uncertain of him in this strange mood, but when she glanced back from the top of the stairs he was still standing looking up at her retreating figure, the glass clenched in his hand.

The oddly vulnerable look she glimpsed momentarily in his eyes brought her breath to a sharp halt ... it was almost as if—— But no, she thought bitterly as her footsteps quickened towards the bedroom. It had been nothing more than a male's long-thwarted desire for a woman she had seen in the eyes raised from the hall below.

Only a trick of light had given her the erroneous impression that unexpressed longing, no longer covered, was visible in those brown depths.

CHAPTER EIGHT

To Jan's surprise, Kyle was at the kitchen table nursing a mug of black coffee next morning when she went down to prepare breakfast for Robbie and herself.

His expression was noncommittal and cool as his eyes went over the neat arrangement of her blue-black hair and trim figure clad in lilac sweater and darker purple slacks. He stood up and took a willing Robbie from her to place him in his chair, a soft glow of tenderness lighting the lean darkness of his face when Robbie reached up with transparent adoration and clasped his arms round his neck.

'How would you like to come in the car with me today?' Kyle enquired affably as he settled the small body behind the tray.

'Car?' Robbie, suspecting from the man's smiling face that yet another exciting treat was in store, nodded agreeably. 'Robbie come!'

Kyle's smile faded when his eyes met the question in Jan's. 'I have to go into town, and I thought it might be a chance for you to pick up anything you need there. Snow's forecast for tomorrow, so it could be a while before we get out again.'

Strangely, the thought of being entrapped for an unknown period in the old ranch house held no terrors for Jan. As the days had gone by, so she had begun to admit to herself that she welcomed the role Kyle had thrust her into, whatever his reasons for doing so. She had unlimited time with Robbie, a luxury heretofore unknown to her apart from weekends and a blissful two-week holiday spent solely with her son in a beach cottage on Vancouver Island. It was Kyle who had opened up this wonderland for her and thrown in the additional compensation of providing a father figure for Robbie.

There were even long periods during the day when she could forget that she was here for no other reason than that Kyle desperately wanted a son. Preparing meals with loving, skilful hands as if they were a normal family, knowing that Kyle's appreciation would show in his eyes if not in the politely worded thanks he invariably gave her each evening.

Still she said coolly in answer to his question: 'There's nothing I need, thanks.'

Going to town meant Williams Lake, where Kyle was at least on nodding terms with a large part of the populace and on friendly terms with a daunting number of lifelong acquaintances, many of whom Jan had met just after her marriage. What would be their reaction to the sudden return of the wife of a man they all respected and admired, a wife moreover with a child Kyle was claiming as his own?

But she had reckoned without Kyle's forethought about the situation. While she settled Robbie with his cereal, Kyle went to the stove with the animal-like grace so unusual in a big man and poured coffee for her and a refill for himself, returning to say quietly:

'Sit down and have this while we talk. Robbie's okay for a while.' And when she reluctantly sat, he went on: 'You're thinking that nobody will believe I'm fool enough to accept your child as mine, right?'

She nodded and looked down into her cup, away from the hard businesslike stare he was levelling at her.

'It's only natural that when you look at Robbie you see—Paul,' he clipped, 'but what other people will accept without question is his likeness to me. None of them knows what happened between us, and most of them never met Paul. But in case any of them has a long memory, we can move Robbie's birth-date back a month. It won't make any difference to him in the long run.'

Jan gasped, her eyes closing in pain as her fingers clenched round the mug. The irony of it rose up like bitter gall in her throat. She had moved Robbie's birthday ahead a month so that Kyle wouldn't suspect the truth, and now Kyle himself was suggesting the opposite so that his friends would accept the child as his!

'No,' she choked, opening her eyes and looking wildly around as if seeking escape from the mesh of lies she had woven for herself. 'I can't let you——'

Misunderstanding her motive, he interrupted bleakly: 'I know it's not easy for you to deny his real father, but Paul's dead, Jan. Don't you think he'd want his son to have the name, the settled home, of his best friend?'

Jan shook her head hopelessly and covered her face with her hands, feeling the difficult tears warm against them. A long-drawn sob she was powerless to prevent burst from her throat.

'Mommy?' Robbie asked uncertainly, and she rose blindly from the table to take refuge at the sink while she wiped her eyes and blew her nose. Vaguely she heard Kyle's voice speaking gently to Robbie, then he was beside her, turning her away from the window to look into the troubled brown of his eyes.

'I'm sorry I had to bring it up, Jan,' he said softly, 'and I promise I won't mention Paul again after today.' He paused, searching her face with a tenderness that sent her heart plummeting to the depths. 'It might be better for you, too, if you could try to put thoughts of the past out of your mind and think of Robbie's future instead of—other things that can never be again.'

Was he still talking about Paul, or was he trying to tell her that the love between them could never be renewed? Something in his voice, the pain of regret, perhaps, indicated the latter, but his face betrayed no sign of his exact meaning. Suddenly weary, Jan pulled away from the hands he had laid lightly on her shoulders and walked over to the stove to prepare the rest of Robbie's breakfast.

'All right, Kyle, I won't think of things that can never be,' she said tightly.

He said nothing for a moment or two, then seemed to inject a note of briskness into his voice as he went back to the table.

'Good. A start would be for you to come with me today. There must be things you need—fresh produce at the supermarket, warmer clothes for Robbie and yourself, gifts for Christmas.'

'I don't have that much money,' she told him briefly, reaching for a pan to scramble eggs in.

Anger edged his voice as he directed it to her back: 'I wasn't expecting you to pay for anything. I'm capable of supporting my—family.'

'Even if your "family" exists only for a few weeks?'

Robbie's high-voiced chatter, directed to no one in particular, sounded loud in the ensuing silence.

'I'll take my chances on that,' Kyle said quietly then and went to take his jacket and shrug his broad shoulders into it. 'I have a couple of things to see to, but I'll be back in an hour.'

The silence he left after striding out of the house was far more potent than the one preceding it.

'We'll have to buy a proper car seat for Robbie,' Kyle remarked with a frown as the station wagon's wheels slid on unmelted ice for the second time, in spite of the heavy gauged snow tyres he had fitted. Jan, clutching Robbie's sturdy figure with protective arms, glanced briefly over at Kyle and stilled the snappish response on her lips. Under the frown was a look that expressed only too clearly his deep longing for the family he believed could never really be his.

'Yes,' she agreed quietly. 'There's never been a need for one before. I—I couldn't afford to buy and run a car.'

Her eyes dropped to his brown hands on the wheel and saw the knuckles grow whiter as his grasp tightened.

'Was it—very bad for you, Jan?'

'It could have been worse,' she said, a shrug in her voice. 'Don was—wonderful. I don't think I'd have survived without him.'

'Why didn't you——?' he burst out in an anguished voice, cutting himself off when Robbie struggled upright on Jan's lap and pointed to the animals grazing at either side of the road.

'Cows!' he said excitedly. 'Lots of cows!'

'Yes, darling, they're Daddy's co——'

Stricken, Jan's eyes met Kyle's above Robbie's dark head. How treacherously easy it had been to use that word! Kyle had noticed her natural use of it, she knew, although his eyes were now narrowed on the road ahead.

'I—I'm sorry,' she apologised haltingly. 'It's just that——'

'Don't be sorry,' he returned briefly. 'It's what I hope he'll call me if you decide to stay. Anyway,' he turned his head to give her a stiff smile, 'I like it.'

Jan subsided into her seat again, responding to Robbie's chatter abstractedly as the car sped on its way to town. Kyle had said he liked to be called 'Daddy' —how deep would his hatred for Jan go if he ever discovered that Robbie had every right in the world to call him that?

'Well, by all that's wonderful! Jan! When did you get back?'

The speaker was a tall and elderly, grizzle-haired rancher Jan remembered clearly from the time Kyle had introduced her as his bride. Bill Flannery and his wife Deirdre were as close neighbours in the opposite direction as the Pearson place to the west. They had been delighted by Kyle's marriage and with the bride he had chosen—Deirdre had confided to Jan not long after their meeting that, contrary to general opinion in the area, she and Bill had never thought of Elena as the right wife for Kyle.

'Not that she isn't a fine girl in many ways,' she had hastened to add, 'but there's always been a kind of coolness about Elena, a hardness Kyle might have found hard to live with—goodness knows, he's had enough of that from his grandmother! I shouldn't be talking this way, but I just wanted you to know how happy we are that Kyle found you, you're just right for him.'

Now, with Bill staring in disbelief at her, Jan could only conjecture what their reaction had been to her sudden disappearance. That they didn't blame her for deserting the man they had known and been fond of all his life was evident in Bill's smiling light blue eyes.

'Wait till I tell Deirdre, she'll be that pleased she won't know what to do with herself!'

He put out a brawny hand, but when Jan took it tentatively he pulled her forward and hugged her hard, his voice unsteady when he put her away a moment later. 'Deirdre knew you wouldn't stay away for ever,' he said gruffly. 'If two people were ever meant for each other, she's always saying, it's Kyle and Jan.'

'Thanks, Bill,' Jan managed a smile, and if it was wistful he appeared not to notice. They were standing in the aisle of a department store where Jan had been searching for small gifts for the ranch employees and their families who would be returning a few days before Christmas. In spite of herself, Bill's welcoming hug, so freely given, had sent a warm glow through her.

'Now you two have got to come over and see us,' he enthused. 'That wife of mine won't be content until she's seen you for herself.'

'That would be nice,' Jan murmured, overwhelmed by memories of happy evenings at the older couple's comfortable ranch home where Kyle and Jan had been made as welcome as their own sons and their wives. 'Maybe we can——'

She stopped, puzzled as Bill's eyes widened to a spot behind her head and colour ebbed from his lined face.

'Well, my God!' he breathed shakily, and stared so hard that Jan turned her head and saw Kyle, Robbie settled comfortably on his left arm, bearing down on them. Robbie was contemplating a gigantic lollipop clutched in one chubby hand, satisfaction evident in his absorption.

'Hi, Bill,' Kyle said with a shade too much heartiness. 'I see you've met Jan.'

Bill seemed speechless, his eyes glued to Robbie's contented figure on the younger man's arm. There was condemnation in their light blue when he at last tore them from the boy and turned them on Jan.

'You've kept Kyle's boy away from him all this time?'

'I—he's—we——'

'The fault was as much mine as Jan's,' Kyle came to her rescue smoothly, his free arm reaching round her thick Indian sweater to pull her to him. 'We had a misunderstanding, but now everything's fine. We're together again—with our son, Robbie.'

Bill looked bewilderedly from one to the other of the three before him and scratched his wiry hair before saying: 'That must have been some misunderstanding!—but I'm glad to know everything's fixed up now.' He shook his head. 'Deirdre will never believe this, not in a million years.'

When his eyes fixed again on Jan's with a puzzled cast to them, Kyle put in: 'Well, why don't you bring her over to see for herself?' He looked lovingly down at Jan. 'We've been thinking of having a party to celebrate, haven't we, honey?'

'What? Oh, yes,' she ad-libbed belatedly, her mind numbed by Bill's unquestioning acceptance of Robbie as Kyle's son. If he, who had known Kyle all his life, accepted that fact unquestioningly, how long would it be before Kyle himself recognised the truth?

'We'd thought next week,' he now lied, his arm firming like a steel band round her jacket. 'Wednesday, wasn't it, sweetheart?'

Jan felt faint suddenly. 'Yes. Yes, Wednesday.'

'Well, I just know Deirdre's not going to contain herself till then,' Bill snorted disgustedly. 'Tell you what, why don't you all come over Sunday afternoon and stay for supper? That way I won't get my head bitten off by my wife, and there's a couple of things I want to show you, Kyle.'

'Fine with me—how about you, Jan?'

The slight loosening of his arm round her waist told Jan that Kyle was leaving the decision up to her, and with Bill's expectant eyes on her there was nothing else to do but agree. Besides, it would be wonderful to see Deirdre again. The older woman's warmth and understanding had been the closest Jan had ever come to being mothered.

The two men conversed for a few minutes longer, but at last Kyle's hand was under her elbow guiding her along the aisle. She collected herself enough to look up into his suddenly grim face.

'Was it necessary to invent a party? Surely——'

'It was the quickest way I know of squashing any rumours about Robbie,' he interrupted grimly. He led her to one of the store's exits, pausing when she halted suddenly and faced him.

'You're really old-fashioned, aren't you?' she said with a mocking air of discovery. 'These days, nobody knows or cares——'

'Around here they do. And so do I.' He took her arm again to propel them from the shop, saying when they had reached the penetrating cold of the outer air: 'Let's go and have some lunch, and we can decide what else we need to buy for a party.'

Leaving her no time to object even if she had wanted to, he led her to the hotel on the next corner where the elegant dining room produced a high chair for Robbie and a menu suitable for his years. Kyle ordered Martinis for himself and Jan while they awaited their meal.

Jan's eyes went appraisingly round the half empty dining room, unconsciously searching for familiar faces and giving a faint sigh of relief when she recognised none of the diners. Her thoughts went back to Kyle's reasons for having a party. Tongues wagged far more critically in country areas. Was that why he had never sought a divorce? Why he had wanted her back here although he had no love for her? She became aware of his scrutiny from the other side of the small table and dropped her eyes.

'I'll call a few people tonight and get it over with,' he said tightly, making no toast to their so-called reconciliation before raising the wide lipped glass to his lips.

Once he would have presented the glazed cherry on a stalk to her, smiling indulgently at her childish pleasure in biting into the flavoured roundness with her small white teeth. But then, she sighed, his fingers, brown and supple, would have been entwined with hers above the table, his eyes soft with the promise of love to come when they were alone.

Now the cherry floated aimlessly in the remaining liquid when he set down the glass and clasped his fingers together in an exclusive gesture. As aimless as she herself felt at that moment. She cleared her throat.

'Who were you thinking of inviting?' she asked with assumed calmness.

He shrugged. 'The Trevors, the Beaudoins, the Davises—Elena and her mother, of course.'

'Of course.' Jan's lashes formed a screen over her eyes for a moment as she played with the cherry in her glass before levelling a straight look across the table. 'Does Elena know about Robbie?' she asked bluntly.

'Yes. I told her the day you brought him here.'

'And what? No hysterics, no——?'

'Elena's not given to hysterics and flights of imagination,' he said curtly, watching as Jan took a bread stick from the basket of rolls on their table and handed it to Robbie, whose interest in the new surroundings was waning rapidly. 'You have the wrong impression about Elena,' he went on in an even tone. 'There's never been any mention of marriage between us, but she's been a great help to me when I've needed a woman's touch around the place.'

Jan's eyes widened in mockery. 'Such male arrogance! You can't really believe that all Elena expected for bestowing her woman's touch was a pat on the head and a grateful thank-you! Or did you express your thanks in a more tangible way?'

Their eyes met and clashed in unspoken antagonism, and it was Jan who dropped her gaze first, her heart pounding suddenly with deep-seated jealousy at the thought of the many hours Elena must have spent alone with Kyle. Hours which she herself had spent nurturing a hatred that had collapsed like a pack of cards at his first touch.

'Let's just say I thanked her in the same way you showed your gratefulness to Don McLeish when he helped you in a time of need,' Kyle threw at her harshly, sitting back when the waitress brought their meal and breaking the ensuing silence to talk noncommittally about the party they were to give the following Wednesday.

It was a conversation Jan participated in only partially. The major portion of her brain was occupied in picturing, in vivid detail, Kyle's method of expressing gratitude to Elena.

True to the forecaster's promise, the snow came in big spreading flakes the following morning, falling from a sky grown leaden from their weight. Softly they settled on the roofs of the ranch buildings, the top sides of the fences, the meadows stretching away on either side of the main house.

Robbie, too excited to eat breakfast, plagued Jan with excited demands to go out until at last she relented and fitted his sturdy body into the larger sized snow suit and warmly lined boots Kyle had insisted on buying for him the day before.

He had also insisted that Jan buy a fur-lined parka

and slim ski pants in a matching shade of red, so that she and Robbie looked, she thought as she closed the front door behind them, like chips from the same block. She had wanted to refuse Kyle's offer in a spurt of independence—for herself, at least—but a glance at his lowering brows and remembrance of the fact that she really had no suitable clothes for the more severe Interior climate made her bite her tongue instead.

Robbie, too young the previous winter to appreciate Vancouver's slight snowfall, stood wrapped in wonder as the dryish flakes fell on his upturned face, frosting his eyelashes and tuft of dark hair visible in front of the fur-edged hood of his snow suit. Her indulgent smile faded when he slowly brought up his arms, mittened palms upright, as if to receive this benediction from heaven as his rightful due.

This world was his ... a world filled with sometimes arduous work, yet one which nevertheless left time to discover the meaning of life, the oneness in man and nature, the maturing of thought untrammelled by the distractions of a hectic city life.

A sudden bubble of laughter escaped Jan when Robbie darted forward and danced in a circle, trying to catch the elusive flakes in his clumsy mittens. Serious thoughts fled as she caught him up and kissed the cold roses on either cheek before running with him in her arms across the thickening underpad of pristine whiteness until they arrived, Robbie squealing with delight, Jan breathlessly laughing, at the crisscross Cariboo fencing separating the house area from the rest of the ranch.

Starting from the fence, they began to roll a snowball along the ground. The powdery snow had sufficient moisture to let it cling to the ever-growing ball, and before long they had begun to aim it for a spot on the lawn in front of the living room window. But halfway there it had grown so heavily round that their combined weight failed to shift it.

Jan, heaving with all her might against the immovable object, felt her feet slide from under her and she fell across the ball and slid off it on to her back. For a second or two Robbie frowned and looked anxiously down at his mother in that unfamiliar position, then, seeing her impish smile, he bent and scooped handfuls of snow, pelting her face and shoulders with them.

His squeals of excitement mingled with her gasping laughter until a man's voice stilled his arms and made him look questioningly up to a point beyond Jan's head.

'That's no way to treat your mother,' Kyle said with mock gruffness, and Robbie, sensing a reprimand though he didn't quite understand the words, let the latest consignment of snow fall to the ground.

'I don't mind,' Jan said quickly, rolling on to her knees and finding herself lifted easily to her feet until she faced the earth colour of Kyle's parka.

Laughter still lingered in the vivid blue sparkle of her eyes, the deep curve of her full lips, as she looked up into his face. The snow, and the deep circle of white fur edging the hood of her jacket, lent a trans-lucency to her skin, and Kyle's deep-set eyes roved over her cheeks tinged with a healthy pink, her eyes brought to intense violet by the reflected whiteness around her.

His gaze dropped then to the relaxed, generous lines of her mouth, her parted lips revealing a glimpse of small even teeth. She caught the fullness of the lower one between her teeth when his arms tightened round her, drawing her with the naturalness of habit to the tensed long line of his hard body. Even through the thickness of their winter clothing, she could feel the muffled thud of his heart—or was it hers?—the hard thrust of his thighs, and knew as familiar waves of electricity from his nerve ends jolted hers into frantic life that once he would have picked her up at that point and carried her to the house ... to make love to her in the only way possible to assuage the passion de-vouring them ...

But now as his head bent slowly to hers she saw him

blink rapidly, the glazed look in his eyes being replaced with a reluctant recalling of where they were, what was happening. He looked down dazedly at the small hand tugging at his trouser leg.

'Daddy do it. Daddy make a snowman with Robbie. Yes?'

Robbie was looking up into Kyle's face ingratiatingly and Jan felt his arms fall away from her as he bent to pick their child up.

'Yes,' he said with sudden exuberance, 'let's go make that snowman.'

Jan watched as the heavy ball of snow was moved with comparative ease towards the house, feeling very alone and bereft suddenly when Robbie looked up with adoring eyes at Kyle, his mother seemingly forgotten. He wouldn't miss her too much, she thought wistfully, if one day ... But she couldn't contemplate that day yet. Too close was that scene with Kyle, their mindless response to each other that needed very little contact to set it into motion.

Was that all it had ever been, a physical thing between them? She had always thought it was more than that. Their ability to comfort each other in arms more tender than passionate, the dreams and hopes of a future together, the family they would have ...

'Hey, we need some help over here!' Kyle called, interrupting her thoughts, and she moved over through the still falling snow, seeing the deep gleam of happiness in his eyes as he set another smaller snowball on top of the bigger one. How much happier would he be if he knew that the child he played with was his own son?

'We need some gear to make him look right,' he grinned, adding in a lower tone: 'There's an old black jacket of mine in the boot room, would you get it?'

'It's not one you use any more?'

'Not unless I can help it. You might bring a carrot for his nose, we'll find some pebbles for his eyes. Oh, and Jan,' he called after her as she walked away, 'there's an old hat of mine on the shelf over the coat, will you bring that too?'

A reluctant smile curved Jan's lips. 'I think you're enjoying this even more than Robbie.'

'Could be,' he returned, suddenly sober as their eyes met and she turned jerkily away to go into the house.

Later, walking back to the house together when lunch time drew near and the snowman, fat and contented-looking, sported an old Stetson hat, black pebble eyes and carrot red nose, Kyle said in a relaxed voice:

'I'll have to get out the sleigh and fix it up. Robbie would have a lot of fun being pulled around by old Gypsy.'

'Gypsy,' Robbie, on his arm, agreed happily. He had met the old mare on several of his forays into the stables with Kyle.

'In fact, we could pay our visit to Bill and Deirdre on Sunday that way,' Kyle went on musingly.

Jan's nerves felt as if they were strung on very fine wires and she turned in the hall to say snappishly: 'It hardly seems worth going to all that trouble for the short time we'll be here,' yet she felt no satisfaction in the immediate tightening of Kyle's jaw, the dying of light in his eyes.

'Maybe so,' he conceded quietly, 'but I'd like to do it anyway.'

'As you wish. Come on, Robbie, let's wash up for lunch.'

CHAPTER NINE

JAN had to admit that the sleigh idea, put into practice, was a runaway success as far as Robbie was concerned.

In the days before their Sunday visit to the Flannery Ranch he never seemed to tire of being pulled in the small yet elaborate sleigh Kyle had unearthed from one of the barns where it had lain neglected since his own childhood. Gypsy, despite her advanced years, seemed to enjoy the unaccustomed exercise in plodding across the snow-encrusted meadows surrounding the house, as if there was now some purpose in a life that had lately been centred mainly on her food stall in the stables.

Jan, a stranger to horses until Kyle's competent instruction after their marriage, had few misgivings about handling the gentle old mare. The times when Kyle accompanied them became more rare as his attention was taken up by ranch chores, and after a day or two, Jan could even harness Gypsy herself and take the impatient Robbie out across the meadows.

Sleep came more easily at night when, her lungs filled with the fresh air of the outdoors, her body tired from caring for the main house and cooking for the three of them, she drifted off soon after laying her head on the pillow. Inevitably the tranquil rhythm of her life was reflected in the disappearance of the dark smudges under her eyes, the refilling of her curves to a less fragile outline, an added spring to her step as she went about the house.

Kyle brought the sleigh and Gypsy round to the front of the house on Sunday afternoon, and Jan was tinglingly aware of his nearness as he sat beside her on the narrow seat, his body turned to accommodate his broad shoulders, his arm stretched along the seat back behind Jan. His other hand held the reins slackly, and when Robbie expressed his longing to hold them Kyle lifted him easily from Jan's lap to his.

'No, don't pull so hard,' he corrected firmly. 'Hold them like this.' His gloveless fingers adjusted Robbie's grip on the leather straps, and Jan's heart skipped a beat when the child looked up at him anxiously for the nod of approval Kyle gave.

Afterwards, Jan realised that that was the moment she made the decision to stay at Silvercreek, come what may. Robbie needed the firm guiding hand of his father as much as Kyle needed a son to guide.

The thought was still too new to her, however, for her to prevent a flinching away when Kyle's hand, returning to the seat back, brushed her cheek and hair. Although she gazed steadily at Gypsy's ample rump plodding steadily through the snow, she was conscious of Kyle's tightlipped scrutiny and sensed the anger in him.

Silently she pleaded with him for understanding, to give her time to get used to the idea of a loveless marriage, one based on the physical attraction between them and the son she had, the son he wanted. But the Kyle he was now had no understanding, no real warmth of love where she was concerned. Always he would have that picture of her and Paul in each other's arms, would listen to no denials on her part.

'Give it time, Jan,' he said huskily now, as if he had been party to her thoughts. Swiftly she turned her head to look at him and thought she saw a glimpse of the Kyle he hid from all the world except her.

She nodded jerkily in answer, and there was silence between them until they came to the Flannery pastures not long after.

'Daddy's cows?' Robbie piped up, retaining his proud hold on the reins.

'No,' Kyle told him, his voice holding a deep thread of contentment. 'They're Uncle Bill's.'

'Uncle Bill's,' Robbie accepted gravely.

Without seeming to take charge, Kyle directed the willing Gypsy towards the two-storied ranch house that had just come into view. Smaller than Silvercreek, it still had the air of having been there for long years, and Jan remembered the cosy feeling of the house that had sheltered Bill and Deirdre and their three sons.

Deirdre awaited them on the narrow front porch, Bill towering behind her, his face wreathed in smiles. The older woman's eyes looked first at Jan with a trembling smile, then lifted to Robbie borne high on Kyle's arm.

'Oh my,' she breathed, 'Bill was right. You could never deny this one as your son, Kyle.'

'I've no intention of doing that, Deirdre,' he said with a tight laugh.

Deirdre hugged Jan, her eyes misty, and made no bones about taking a willing Robbie into her arms and leading the way into the house.

'I'll see to the horse,' Kyle said to Bill, and the older man turned immediately back into the house.

'I'll get my jacket and come with you,' he said. 'Might as well get our tour of inspection over at the same time.'

Jan, feeling like a third wheel, crossed the threshold after him and found Deirdre in the living room off the square hall divesting Robbie of his bulky outer garments.

'Oh, Jan,' she looked up to say, her fingers still busy with zippers and boots with the long expertise of mother and grandmotherhood, 'I can't begin to tell you how happy I am things have turned out this way for you and Kyle.'

'Thank you.' Jan felt the prick of tears at the back of her eyes and occupied her hands in taking off her own jacket and ear-hugging knitted white hat. Deirdre took them from her as she went to the hall closet with

Robbie's snow suit, and when she came back she smiled brightly at the child and took his hand in hers.

'Come along, Robbie, we'll see what we can find for you to play with while Mommy and I have a little talk.'

Jan's heart sank while Deirdre led Robbie to wide cupboards under the bookshelves. Somehow she didn't want to discuss her return to Silvercreek even with Deirdre, whose understanding she could count on.

But when Robbie was settled on the floor nearby with an assortment of toys and books kept, Jan suspected, for the grandchildren who visited the old homestead frequently, Deirdre came and sat in the armchair close to Jan's corner of the sofa. Her neatly waved greying hair framed a face lined lightly with the joy and tribulation she had known in her life, hazel eyes brimming with the pleasure she felt in the presence of Jan and Robbie.

'Jan dear, I'm not going to pry,' she began. 'Everybody around here has had a theory as to why you and Kyle—split up. I've had my own thoughts, of course, but'—she smiled mistily down at the absorbed Robbie—'all I can think of right now is that you're together again where I've always known you should be, and that you have a beautiful son to cement your relationship.'

'Yes,' Jan got out with difficulty. 'Kyle—loves Robbie.'

'He loved you first,' Deirdre said gently. 'And however much a man likes to know he has a son, an heir, it's the woman in his life who has real importance for him.'

'It's—very important to Kyle that he—has a son ...'

'Of course it is. Every man wants to feel that what he's worked hard to achieve will one day belong to his own flesh and blood. But in the day-to-day living, in having a wife who loves him for the man he is, he needs a wife to come home to, a woman to share his life with.'

'There are lots of women who could have shared his life,' Jan fenced.

'Lots of women who would have *liked* to share his life,' Deirdre corrected firmly. 'Elena for one. Oh, I know there's been talk about the amount of time she's been spending over at Silvercreek since you left, but this is the first time in three years that I've seen Kyle looking happy the way he used to be. And that's not due entirely to having a son of his own, Jan.'

'Perhaps not,' Jan agreed, although privately she knew otherwise.

'You'll see, dear,' Deirdre said comfortingly. 'There hasn't been anyone else for you either, has there?' Her hazel eyes looked kindly but shrewdly into Jan's.

'No.'

'You'll see,' Deirdre promised, her eyes twinkling. 'You'll have more babies, and——'

'For heaven's sake, Deirdre, let the girl get back here for five minutes before you're saddling her with half a dozen more kids,' Bill grumbled amiably from the doorway leading to the back regions of the house. Kyle, minus his jacket, stood directly behind him and Jan wondered in sudden panic how much of the conversation he had heard. There was an odd gleam in his eye when he came further into the room, although his attention was immediately diverted when Robbie engagingly held up the toys Deirdre had given him for Kyle's inspection.

The two men had beer while Jan and Deirdre drank the tea the older woman prepared, Robbie leaving the fascinating new toys long enough to drink the fresh creamy milk and eat the home-baked cookies Deirdre gave him. Under the friendly unexciting chatter Jan relaxed and even let herself feel pride in Kyle's staunch defence of his decision to turn some of his timber lands over to the lumber company.

'Sure, I've always felt the way you and Tom Henderson and a lot of the old-timers felt about letting the lumber companies into the forest land. But after reading and thinking a lot about it, I couldn't see where we'd go wrong in opening up the timber to the saw

men. I'm a cattle man primarily, so any method that
gives me more grazing space is the right one for me. I
won't deny that it's been profitable to let the lumber
company in, but to me that's a side issue. I'm more
interested in how many more head of cattle I can run
when they're through.'

Bill agreed, albeit reluctantly, and conversation
flowed in other directions while they partook of the
expertly cooked meal Deirdre provided a little later.
Jan helped Deirdre with the dishes in her country
farmhouse kitchen after dinner, and when they at last
returned to the living room it was to find the two men
still deep in ranch conversation and Robbie fast asleep
on the sofa.

'Kyle, we should go and get Robbie to bed,' she said
hesitantly, surprised when he rose at once.

'Okay, honey. I'll get his things.'

Inexplicably, Deirdre patted Jan's arm and whispered: 'You see? He hasn't taken his eyes from you all
through dinner. You've no cause to worry about anyone else, Jan dear.'

'No . . . no, of course not.'

Jan's fingers seemed clumsy somehow as she zipped
the still sleeping Robbie into his suit and tugged on
his fleecy-lined boots. By the time she had made him
ready Kyle was standing by to take him from her while
she donned her own warm jacket and white hat.

'You'll need your hood up too,' he told her when
they stood on the porch and felt the crisp coldness of
the outside air. As if he didn't trust her to do it herself
he lifted his free hand and flipped her hood up round
her face.

To her surprise, Gypsy stood patiently by the white-
painted garden fence, harnessed securely to the sleigh,
which was outlined in clear coolness by the light of a
brilliant moon rising high in a dark blue sky.

Kyle chuckled as they walked out to the sleigh after
saying their goodnights. 'Bill has his own method of
signalling to Ralph, his general man, when visitors are

ready to leave. He does it by lights, I think, but whether it's a car or a sleigh, it's always ready and facing in the right direction.'

'They're a sweet couple,' Jan murmured as he helped her into the narrow seat.

'Yes,' he said briefly, and went round the back of the sleigh to install himself and Robbie on the seat beside her.

Without thinking, Jan picked up the reins and clucked at the willing Gypsy to start off for home, and in another moment heard the soft swish of the runners through moon-gilded snow. There was a last wave and shouted goodbyes to the elderly couple still on the porch, then Jan relaxed against the arm Kyle had placed behind her head on the seat back. She had to lean back to see the cool velvet of the sky studded with the brilliance of diamond-sharp stars. The moon cast an ethereal glow over the pines climbing the hills on either side and she shivered, pressing further into the down-clad arm behind her.

'Cold?' Kyle asked, and brought down his arm to circle her shoulders and pull her gently towards him.

'No, not really. It's just so—so big, isn't it?'

'Mm-hm, it's a big country all right. Can you imagine how the native people used to feel about it? All this space, and not a white man in sight.'

She twisted her head up to look at his shadowed face. 'It sounds as if you think that was a good thing—I wouldn't have expected that of *you*.'

'Because I'm a white man and I own so many acres of it now?' She felt his shrug. 'The country has grown and developed under white men, but I still have the odd twinge of nostalgia for the simple life the Indians knew once. Simple in some ways, but survival in hard conditions was tough. Not only in finding enough to eat and clothe themselves, but battling the diseases brought in from other parts of the world. Measles alone wiped out whole villages once.'

'I'm glad you care,' she said softly.

'Are you?'

Her face was still raised to his and she saw the deeply shadowed eyes fall to her lips, his arm tighten round the sleeping Robbie as he bent his head to touch his mouth to hers. The warm mingling of their breath thawed the coldness of their lips. Gypsy, needing no guidance, plodded steadily on towards home and her warm barn. The cosily wrapped child slept on in his father's arm. The kiss deepened, rousing in Jan all the raw desire she had forced into numbness although there was a quality of gentleness about Kyle's lips, as if he held himself in check in order to woo her into acceptance of his underlying passion. His head lifted from the soft cling of her lips.

'Tonight,' he said huskily, bending his head again to kiss tantalisingly her cheeks and eyes, her temples, 'when we get home, will you ask me into your room? I said I wouldn't come without an invitation, remember?'

An invitation from his wife, he had said, and she had thought he meant Elena. Memory stirred and started her pulses racing for another reason as panic suddenly swept through her. The cold savagery of his fury that first night of her return rose up to obscure the moon-shadowed tenderness of his face now, replacing it with the image of his burning eyes lit with the deep inner hatred he felt for her then.

Nothing had changed, except that now he wanted her to stay here as his wife because she was the key to his possession of the son he craved. He was a physical man—it would mean very little to him to make love to a woman he considered attractive if he could achieve his ends that way.

'No,' she whispered, pulling out of his arm and sitting up straight beside him. 'Let's—give it time, as you said.'

'No?'

There was shocked puzzlement in the single word, then his voice hardened. 'What do you mean, no? You want it as much as I do, admit it!'

'I can't, Kyle. Without love——'

'Love!' The disgusted exclamation moved the hair touching her cheek under her hat. Her jacket hood had fallen back on her shoulders. 'Is that what you had going with Paul? Well, Paul's dead, Jan, and you're very much alive, so it's useless your trying to build a sexless shrine around his memory! You need proof? I'll give it to you!'

His hand grasped her hair at the back of her head under the cap and pulled it savagely until her face was raised to his again. His mouth cut off her pained gasp as it ground against her parted lips and teeth. Shockwaves washed over her with the memory of that other night when he had taken her in hatred and anger. Midnight blackness covered her vision for unaccountable seconds, and she felt herself whirling away into a vortex of fear and horror.

And then she was surfacing, reaching for the air made suddenly available by the abrupt lift of his head. But as her lungs filled and expanded with the biting coldness of icy air, clearing her brain, she made the startling discovery that her fingers were entwined in the thickest part of Kyle's hair. Moreover that she was unable to resist the pressure those fingers exerted to bring his mouth down to hers again; it was as if she had no power to control the ravaging need stampeding through her veins ... the need to be one with, to be possessed by, to be *loved* by this man.

'You see?' he whispered shakily against her lips, kissing them once lightly before lifting his head as realisation struck him. 'We're home.'

Jan, too, felt the stillness, heard the restless snort of the faithful Gypsy, and knew that they had come home. Home to Silvercreek.

Kyle rose in one lithe movement and stepped down from the sleigh, holding Robbie easily in one arm while he turned to help Jan down from the step. His arm remained round her waist, and even through the thickness of her jacket she felt the iron and steel of it against her flesh.

'We'll give it time,' he said, quietly serious. 'But not too much time.'

She could only nod and follow him along the path to the house. However much time he gave her, she knew it would do nothing to quench the fires he had reawakened in her. And at that moment she didn't care whether it was all-encompassing love or just the physical expression of a passionate man's desire for the woman who happened to be his wife.

Jan expected embarrassment, or at least an air of constraint, between them after the emotionally fraught ride back from the Flannery ranch, but if there was anything of either quality it was confined to Jan herself.

Kyle was as noncommittal as always when he returned as usual the next morning to drink coffee while she and Robbie ate breakfast. The only difference came in the evening when Robbie was in bed and they sat before the crackling fire with coffee after dinner.

Since the night when he had shown her the renovated room that had once been his grandmother's, Kyle had confined himself to a pre-dinner whisky and coffee during the evening, with an occasional nightcap before he and Jan retired to their respective bedrooms.

Nothing of this had changed, but on the Monday evening there was a more relaxed atmosphere as they sat companionably in the living room. Kyle spoke quietly about the ranch operation and his plans for the future, and seemed to listen to Jan's murmured replies as if they mattered to him. With a strange sense of suspended animation, Jan let this undreamed-of togetherness flow over her, recognising it without questioning the deeper meaning it could have.

Until Tuesday, the night before the party Kyle had

arranged. Robbie had seemed feverish as she prepared
him for bed, his hair damp across his moist forehead.
Kyle looked up when she at last went downstairs and
crossed slowly to the hearth area.

'Something wrong? Is he all right?'

'I think so,' she frowned, and sat tiredly in the chair
opposite. The combination of beginning preparations
for the party and coping with an increasingly cranky
child had exhausted her. 'It could be he's sickening for
a cold.' Her eyes went round the room and she gave an
involuntary shiver. 'We're so far away from everything
here.'

'We can get to a doctor in a matter of minutes by
plane,' Kyle assured her quietly, catching her meaning immediately. 'If you're still worried about him in
the morning I can phone the clinic then and tell them
what his symptoms are.'

'Thank you.' Comforted, yet feeling suddenly shy
under the scrutiny of his deep-set eyes, Jan rose. 'I'll
see to the dishes.'

'They're done.'

She stopped close to his chair and looked down into
his raised face. 'There's no need for you to do them,
that's my job, isn't it?'

'Is that all it is to you, Jan?—a job?' Kyle stood
with a sudden movement that made her take a stumbling step backward.

'I'm here as your temporary housekeeper—what else
would you call it?' she put quietly, arching her neck
to look up into brown eyes that held a similar sparkle
to the one in her own.

'You're still my wife, Jan.'

The quiet words were accompanied by a firm hand
reaching round her back to pull her against the flat
hardness of his chest. Panicked, her heart raced and felt
the answering pound of his as their bodies reacted to
the close contact.

Jan lowered her eyes to the undone shirt at his

throat, to the point where the steely column of his neck began. 'I—I haven't been your wife for—a long time.'

'That can be remedied.'

Her eyes lifted to his, seeing there the hungrily intent look of a man close to the limits of physical endurance. 'Without love, Kyle? I—I couldn't.'

'There would be love on one side,' he clipped, and she knew which side that would be when his arms grew slack round her. She shook her head.

'It wouldn't work,' she said bitterly, and challenged him with her eyes. 'You want Robbie very badly for your son, don't you?'

A frown creased its way between his eyes as he hesitated. 'Yes,' he admitted slowly, and seemed about to add something more when Jan interrupted him.

'Then don't ask for more now,' she said with a crispness that surprised herself. 'You said we'd give it time as far as you and I are concerned——'

'Time?' he laughed harshly. 'Take all the time in the world!'

His face seemed carved from granite, his lips clamped to a thin line when he turned to stride past her, his heels beating a furious tattoo on the polished floor as he bulldozed his way to the study.

The door slammed behind him, and the crackling of the logs in the fireplace was suddenly loud in Jan's ears. Trembling, she stumbled round to sink into the sofa's deep cushions. Would it have been so wrong to succumb to the mindless need she felt to be Kyle's wife again in deed as well as name? Wrong to hope that their union would result in the growth of a new, a deeper love than they had known once? A love with a firm underpinning of trust which would enable her to tell him the truth at last? Sighing, she pulled herself up wearily and walked to the stairs on shaky legs.

The turned wood of the banister rail felt firm under her fingers as she ascended. Firm and strong, in the same way Kyle was, as this house with its long history of sheltering and providing comfort for generations of Masters. A roof that should protect the youngest Masters of all ...

Jan struggled from the depths of a dreamless sleep, hearing her name called urgently in a man's voice, a child's wails coming to her from a distance. Blinking, she stared straight up into Kyle's drawn features.

'Kyle?' she murmured dazedly. 'What——?'

'It's Robbie,' he said tersely. 'He's been crying for quite a while. I came in to see if I could quiet him, but he wants you.'

Her eyes went uncomprehendingly down over the short dark robe he wore, noting unconsciously that he still apparently wore no pyjamas to bed. Renewed sobs from Robbie galvanised her into action and she threw back the covers and leapt from the bed, not even bothering in her haste to reach for her slippers.

'I'll see to him!' she called sharply as Kyle went ahead of her into the small room adjoining, scarcely noticing his tightened jaw as she hurried forward to switch on the small table lamp beside the child's bed. 'It's all right, darling, Mommy's here.'

Murmuring soothingly, she lifted the sturdy body from the bed and sat on the small side chair, stroking the dark hair back from Robbie's forehead and holding him tightly against her breast with the other arm.

'Want drink, Mommy,' he hiccuped, and her eyes went to the empty water glass by the bed.

'I'll get it,' Kyle said from the door. 'Is orange juice okay?'

He disappeared almost before her nod, and Jan returned her attention to Robbie, wrapping a blanket from his bed round him and rocking him gently.

When Kyle reappeared with the glass of chilled orange juice the child was almost asleep again and lay down contentedly after swallowing just a sip or two. Jan stood looking down at him for long minutes after she had tucked the blankets round him, then, satisfied that he slept, straightened and reached out a hand for the light.

A movement from the other side of the room brought her head round sharply, her hair swinging in silken threads round her face and shoulders. She had forgotten Kyle for the moment, presuming he had gone back to bed after bringing the drink, but he was there outlined against the doorway.

In his eyes was a look that stopped the breath in her throat, a look that made her conscious suddenly of the filminess of her nightdress, of the curves revealed in the light as it shone through the thin peach-coloured nylon. Her hand froze on the switch as their eyes locked and held for interminable moments. It was as if they communicated with an eloquence mere words could never convey, in a language that spoke of remembered passion between them, fires that still smouldered deep within each of them. The flames from that fire had ignited and flared deep in the brown of his eyes, and there seemed an inevitability about the way he waited for her to switch off the lamp and come to him.

In the short time it took Jan to extinguish the light and walk on leaden bare feet to the doorway where he towered in dark relief against the stronger light from the master bedroom her mind had reasoned, with a coolness remote from the molten warmth spreading through her, that this time she would put up no resistance. The pull of her love for Kyle was too strong for that. And an infallible age-old instinct told her that a rekindling of the love he had once had for her could be fanned to life more readily in this basic, physical way ...

'Jan.'

Her name on his lips, spoken with a ragged hoarseness, held more of demand than question, the same demand that was in his firm closing of the door between the rooms before turning back to gather her against him in a possessive moment that left her no room to object.

Not that the tremors shaking her body would allow for objections anyway ... her head dropped on the hard warm surface of his chest where his robe parted over darkly meshed hair, only the firmness of his arms round her prevented her collapse at his feet in an ignominious heap.

'Jan?'

This time there was question in the husky way he said her name, his fingers gentle yet firm under her chin, raising the nervously widened blue of her eyes to the flames leaping in his. His hand behind her back seared through the gauze of her nightdress to the tender flesh beneath, and her body was unresisting as he drew it closer to the curve of his.

The slow bend of his head brought his lips not to her mouth but to the pulse at her temple, to her closed eyelids in turn, and then she felt their warm seeking at her throat, at the deep cleft between breasts made taut by a desire as potent as that expressed in the lean body pressing hers to its downward arch.

'Kyle,' she murmured, wanting yet dreading the feel of those lips on hers, seeking and possessing as they had long ago, when he loved her too. Her hands swept from the tangled growth on his chest to the smoothly muscled hardness of his back. Had he undone the loose tie on his robe or had she?—it didn't matter. Nothing mattered but the longing to meld her body to the sleek hardness of his. His mouth came down then with such suddenness on hers that she reeled and clutched the sinewy flesh under her hands. Wanting, needing, all at once became possible—inevitable—as mouth answered to mouth, yielding softness to insistent hardness ... she felt herself lifted, carried a few steps ...

The velvet coolness of sheet beneath her gave way to torrid warmth, a warmth that bathed her in its sweetness while sending the sting of awareness of thigh against thigh, crushing chest against tender curve of breast, mouth demanding against ardently parted lips

... her skin felt like shot silk where his hands, roughened by work, touched and stroked abrasively ... cajoling, demanding the response that now flooded from her and drowned her own senses in the delirious joy of giving, receiving ...

CHAPTER TEN

'KYLE?'

Sated, hate transformed into the love she had known existed under the thin layer of darkness beneath her outer surfaces, Jan spoke into the darkness of the bedroom.

Although it wasn't entirely dark. The beginning glimmer of morning was already sending probing fingers through the partially drawn curtains at the windows, giving a shadowy reality to the dresser and chest of drawers, revealing the dark pool of Kyle's robe and her abandoned peach nightdress cast on the floor haphazardly.

But what she had to say must be spoken to the anonymity of the blurrily outlined ceiling. Not to the eyes that had blazed with desire a few short minutes ago.

Kyle's arm tightened round her and she heard him sigh, deeply and luxuriously, from beside her.

'Kyle?' she whispered tentatively. 'Kyle, I have to tell you. It's been such a strain not telling you till now, but ... I thought you hated me, and that you'd take Robbie from me. Not that you wouldn't have been justified in doing that because ... well, you see, darling, Robbie is your son.'

Her voice became still, her breath silenced in her throat, as she waited for his reaction. But there was no drawing away of his arm, no shrinking of his relaxed body from hers. Jan's voice thickened with emotion when she went on in a whisper: 'I never loved Paul, Kyle. There's never been anyone but you ... and now that I know you love me too, we can be the family we were meant to be. You, me, and Robbie ...'

Now his lack of response piqued her, but as she turned her head to his on the pillows her ears caught the steady rhythm of his breathing even as her eyes saw that his were closed, the normally stern lines of his strong face relaxed in formless contentment. He was asleep! He had heard not one word of her confession, the admission she had screwed up her courage to make!

Swiftly her head swivelled back to the ceiling. Perhaps it was better that he hadn't heard. In all the hurried whispers her ears had barely caught, not one phrase had voiced his love for her. She had been left in no doubt as to his need of her, his deep desire for her ... but, she realised now with trembling misgiving, there had been nothing to indicate that a more encompassing love entered into their coming together. That would have to wait until the new relationship had settled down, had developed recognisable guidelines apart from driving physical needs ...

Jan slept, Kyle's arm protectively across her, but when she woke the comforting presence had gone from her back and Robbie's plaintive calling pierced the gossamer dreams that had filled her sleep. It was late, she saw as she slid from the high bed and picked up her nightdress draped discreetly across the end of the bed. Kyle must have done that when he rose earlier, she thought as she slipped its frothy folds over her head and felt for her slippers with bare toes, a smile lifting the well-kissed outline of her mouth. How had he looked when he rose from beside her? Satisfied? Happy?

Contentment flowed in a bubbling stream through her veins as she went in to pick up the complaining Robbie. She had drawn on her blue wool robe over her nightdress, and he clung to that as he belligerently demanded breakfast.

'Robbie hungry, Mommy,' he accused.

'I know, darling, Mommy slept too long,' she

soothed, running an exploratory palm over his forehead and feeling pleased at its coolness. Evidently the fever had been a twenty-four-hour thing, but she nevertheless dressed him warmly before taking him down to the big kitchen. She left her own dressing until later.

Settling Robbie in his chair with a bowl of cereal and thick creamy milk from the Silvercreek milking cow, she set about preparing the rest of his breakfast, sipping gratefully on a lukewarm mug of coffee left from Kyle's breakfast while a fresh brew filled the kitchen with its aromatic scent.

She had thought her ears were alert to the slightest sound of Kyle's return, but when he did come she failed to hear the uncharacteristically quiet opening of the door or his approach until his arms slid round her from behind and his face buried itself in the dark spray of hair at her nape.

'Kyle,' she breathed, turning in his arms so that she could look up at him, all that was in her heart beaming from her eyes. She caught a brief glimpse of the leaping glow in his eyes as he bent his head to kiss her with lips that were hard and still held the coolness of Cariboo air. 'Robbie,' she murmured, pulling away slightly to glance apprehensively at the small boy who was totally preoccupied with food at that moment.

'He'll have to get used to seeing me greet his mother properly in the morning—and at other times,' Kyle returned huskily, sparing no attention for the absorbed Robbie as he bent to kiss her again.

A pang shot through Jan even while she accepted the mouth he pressed to hers. How much longer would it be before she could tell him that Robbie was his son as well as hers?

The water bubbled over furiously in the pan boiling two eggs and she turned with a small exclamation to the stove, partially relieved when Kyle left her and went to pour coffee from the freshly brewed pot.

'Do you need any help getting ready for the party

tonight?' he asked when she settled at the table with her boiled egg and side plate of toast. 'It's a pity the ranch wives aren't here, they'd have been only too pleased to help with things.'

'It's all right, I'll manage. I made a start on the baking yesterday.' It was hard for her to understand the shyness that filled her now in his presence, although a few hours before their intimacy had been complete. 'If you could take Robbie out with you a little later it would help. Whatever was wrong with him last night seems to be better now.'

'I could say the same thing for myself,' he murmured, capturing her hand in the warm strength of his and raising it to his lips, looking searchingly into her eyes as he did so and bringing a warm flood of colour to her cheeks. 'You made me very happy last night, Jan,' he went on softly. 'You won't go away now?'

Jan hesitated for a second or two before whispering: 'No,' and she pulled her hand away from his to curve it round the cooling oval of brown-shelled egg. She could take his question in two ways, she mused as she dipped her spoon into the dark yellow yolk. His love-making had either been designed expressly with the purpose of persuading her to stay with the son he craved, or it had been a spontaneous outpouring of physical need dammed up for too long.

But did it matter which reason was the right one? Time and the strength of her own love could weave the tapestry of a newer, stronger love between them.

The day flew by in a flurry of preparation. There was a variety of salad dishes to be made up, but they were left until the afternoon. Meanwhile, Jan busied herself with dough for bread rolls and the boning of chicken pieces to be cooked in a tangy sauce and served hot on this cold winter night. As well, there would be ham from their own Silvercreek pigs, the ranch hens supplying eggs for devilling.

Jan had almost the whole day to make her preparations, Kyle having taken Robbie out with him during the morning and the afternoon hours free while Robbie slept soundly, full of fresh air and the excitement of being out with the ranch men all morning. Tiny and Shortstop, the two inseparables who had worked for Kyle for years, treated the small boy like a crown prince, an honour he received as no more than his due, and Tom Henderson rounded out the picture as the grandfather figure Robbie loved to be with.

Dinner was a hurried affair that evening, taken in the kitchen because the long dining room table had been laid with stiff white linen, gleaming cutlery placed conveniently at one end for the buffet type meal later, and a three-holder candelabrum at either end of the table.

'Leave that,' said Kyle, coming up behind Jan as she began filling the steel-lined sink with hot water to do the dishes. 'I'll see to it while you get Robbie ready. I'd like him to be here, even in his pyjamas, when everyone arrives.'

Implied in his quietly toned words was his wish to publicly claim Robbie as his son, and Jan bit her lip as she turned back to the sink. Soon she would tell him the truth—but not now, when there was barely an hour before the guests would begin to arrive. 'If you bring him down, I'll take care of him while you get ready,' he offered.

'But what about you?' she objected, her heart sinking at the prospect of greeting the natural curiosity of their neighbours without Kyle to back her up.

'I just have to change my clothes, I've already showered. Jan,' he caught her wrist as she put down the towel she had been drying her hands with, 'does it—bother you—that Robbie's the only child you'll have if you stay with me?'

How painful it was for him to utter the words was evident in the hardened line of his jaw, the compression of his well-shaped lips, and Jan's voice caught in a faint sob as she whispered desperately: 'Oh, *Kyle*!'

'I just want to be sure you realise what you'll be facing, that you won't regret it later ...'

Jan stilled his voice with trembling fingers placed on his lips. 'I'll never regret anything, Kyle,' she said unsteadily. 'I only want to be where you are.'

He had refrained from touching her until then, but now his arms circled her and pulled her roughly to him. The warm hardness of his mouth sought and found hers, response flaming immediately along her tautened nerve ends to deaden the pangs of guilt at her deception. Her arms reached round his neck as his kiss deepened with quickening passion, her body curving up to his until a quivering wail from Robbie made her jerk back and stare at her child. The quiver was on his lower lip, too, as he gazed accusingly at Kyle and tears filled his brown eyes.

'Want Mommy,' he sobbed, holding up his arms in a pathetic gesture so that Jan caught her breath quickly and crossed to lift him from the chair.

Kyle came to stand near them, his lazy smile fading when Robbie turned deliberately away from him to bury his face in Jan's neck.

'You see I was right about not letting him sleep in your bed,' Kyle said, a tinge of annoyance in his voice. 'He'd never have let me near it. And if there's one thing this young man has to learn, it's that I'll be sharing your bed and kissing you whenever I feel like it.'

'He's just a baby, Kyle,' Jan soothed the father with her voice and the son with a patting hand on his back. 'Give him time to get used to things he's never seen before.'

There was silence for a few moments apart from the muffled sobs coming from Robbie.

'He's never seen you being kissed by a man?'

Jan eyed him levelly over Robbie's head. 'Not that way, no.'

Another silence, then Kyle's hand reached out to ruffle the back of Robbie's dark hair. 'You'd better start getting ready, time's running short,' was all he said, but Jan seemed to glimpse a light in his eyes that had not been there before as she turned to leave the kitchen.

What had pleased him so much? Was it that there had been no passionate love scenes in her life, at least not in Robbie's presence?

How right Kyle had been to insist on having Robbie attend the first part of the evening, Jan thought, smiling faintly when she caught sight of the small figure almost lost on a voluminous lap in one of the hearth chairs.

The faint note of censure she had sensed in some of the neighbours had been dissipated rapidly at the sight of Robbie perched easily and familiarly on Kyle's arm. So what, she could almost hear them say, if Jan had walked out on Kyle three years ago? Hadn't she returned and made him proud and happy by presenting him with the son he had wanted for so long?

With one exception, Robbie was accepted without question as Kyle's son. The exception was Elena who, after a first dismayed drawing in of her breath, had worn a faintly sceptical look each time her eyes strayed in his direction. At that moment, scorn curled her lip at the indulgent coos coming from the group of older women seated near the fire.

'I've never seen a child so like his father,' said Mamie Philips, on whose lap Robbie sat, smiling indulgently down into his upturned face. 'I remember Kyle very well at this age, and there's not a bit of difference between them. Robbie's maybe a little darker, but then Jan is too.' Her smile deepened. 'You know I'm talking about your daddy, don't you?'

'Daddy?' Robbie repeated, his head swivelling until he located Kyle, whereupon he grinned and pointed. 'Daddy,' he said with some satisfaction, his previous antipathy towards Kyle forgotten.

Taking advantage of this, Kyle put his drink down

and came to lift Robbie into his arms. 'Yes, and your daddy says it's time for you to go to bed, young man.'

Jan moved quickly when Robbie's brows drew down in a frown at the fatal word, his eyes trying to outstare the level look in Kyle's.

'I'll take him up, Kyle,' she said hurriedly, and received the belligerent-looking Robbie into her arms, noting the unnatural flush on his rounded cheeks. Kyle had followed them to the bottom of the stairs and she said worriedly: 'He looks a little feverish again.'

'Probably all the excitement and fussing he's had,' Kyle returned with faint sympathy, yet his eyes softened as they looked down into the concerned sheen of hers. 'We can take turns checking him after he's asleep.'

Nodding, she smiled up at him, knowing and not caring that eyes were on them from every part of the room. Then from halfway up the carpeted stairs she felt her eyes drawn to where Elena stood with Stu Philips, the son of Mamie and Howard, who had returned for a long vacation from his law practice in Vancouver. A shiver went over Jan at the barely concealed venom in Elena's eyes as she watched mother and son ascend the stairs. Venom flicked to rawness by Kyle's obvious lack of interest in her manoeuvres to corner him privately, so that now she stood sulkily by the one unattached man at the party.

Stu, tall and with straight light brown hair, had become a widower the year before, and from the look in his hazel eyes he would be more than willing to renew and deepen the relationship he and Elena had had years before.

Robbie was fractious when Jan put him to bed, and she wondered if Kyle might be right in his conjecture that too much spoiling tonight had brought about his fever. For the first time in his life she spoke to him sharply, guilt striking her when he stared up at her in amazement, his lower lip trembling.

'Go to sleep, darling,' she said softly, bending to kiss him and feeling the heat in his rounded cheek.

Was Kyle right, or was he sickening for something? Whatever the reason, she sat beside him longer than usual, making sure he was deeply asleep before getting up and stretching, dropping another light kiss on his forehead and leaving the table lamp lit as she tiptoed to the door. She gasped suddenly when she noticed Elena's figure, shown to advantage in clinging pink jersey, watching her from the master bedroom.

'Did you want something?' Jan asked coolly, drawing the door of the small room partly closed behind her.

'Nothing you can supply,' the other girl retorted with unveiled insolence, her mouth turning up in a sneer. 'You really think you're smart, don't you? Passing that child off as Kyle's, when I know that——'

'You know *what*, Elena?' Jan said witheringly, turning to sit at the dressing table and drawing a brush through her loosened black hair, stilling the trembling of her fingers. 'Everyone else down there knows Robbie is Kyle's son—why do you find it so difficult to accept?'

'Everybody down there doesn't know about your affair with Paul Steel,' Elena snapped, moving to stand behind Jan's stiffened form in midnight blue silk that left her shoulders creamily exposed. 'Or that Kyle threw you out because of it! Oh, don't look so shocked, sweetie—do you imagine he didn't tell me all about it? You knew he was desperate to have a son, so you traded on his and Paul's likeness to pass your brat off as his! But how long do you think you can fool a man like Kyle? I wouldn't like to be in your shoes when he finds out the truth!'

Jan slammed the brush down on the hardwood surface before her and turned contemptuously to stare into the contorted face of the other girl. 'That's always been your problem, Elena, hasn't it?' she said slowly. 'You've always wanted to be in my shoes where Kyle's concerned, and you can't accept that he's not interested in you as a woman! Robbie is Kyle's child, make no mistake about that.'

Elena teetered impotently before her for a few

moments then turned and half ran to the door, looking back to say: 'The mistake is yours if you think I'll
let Kyle go on believing——'

'All you'll accomplish is to make a fool of yourself,'
Jan sighed impatiently, but the other girl had already
disappeared.

A burst of laughter from below reminded her that
she should begin to set out the food and she rose with
sudden weariness, wishing that the evening was already
over, that she and Kyle were alone. She would tell him
the truth tonight, whatever happened.

There was no sign of Elena, or of Kyle, when Jan
descended the staircase and she knew that the other
girl had at last succeeded in cornering him in some
remote spot. What would Kyle say to refute the allega-
tion? That he already knew that Robbie wasn't his
son? Or would he preserve what he believed to be an
illusion?

No one noticed Jan, or the slight frown between her
dark brows, as she crossed the living room to the kitchen. Taking the prepared trays and bowls from
pantry and refrigerator and placing them on the wide
serving hatch to the dining room occupied her
thoughts for the next few minutes, so that the faint
swish of the kitchen door opening made no impression
on her consciousness. She started when she turned
from the hatch and found Kyle only a step or two
away.

A stillness about his face, a bleakness deep in his
eyes, made her ask hesitantly: 'You saw Elena? She—
told you what she suspects?'

He nodded.

'What—what did you tell her?'

He shrugged. 'That she's all wrong, that Robbie's—
my son.' His arms reached out for her suddenly and
she found herself held tightly within them, his face
against her hair, his words coming in an anguished
muffle. 'Jan ... Jan, I wish—oh God, how I wish he
was mine!'

Her hands lifted in an instinctive gesture of comfort, stroking the thick short hair at his nape. 'Kyle, there's something I——'

'Come on, you two lovebirds!' Deirdre said from the doorway, holding the door open so that the sounds of people enjoying themselves doubled in intensity. Her motherly blue eyes twinkled. 'You've plenty of time for that later—and the sooner everybody eats, the sooner they'll leave! I came to offer some help, Jan.'

'Yes . . . thanks.'

Jan and Kyle had moved apart at the first sound of Deirdre's voice, and he recovered his equilibrium much quicker than she.

'Well, I'll leave you ladies to it,' he smiled, running a smoothing hand over his hair and looking with bland eyes at Jan. 'Would you like me to check on Robbie?'

'Please,' she said automatically, then turned to Deirdre. 'I've put most of the stuff on the hatch—would you like to set it out on the dining room table while I see to the oven dishes and start the coffee?'

'Surely.' The older silver-haired woman hesitated before leaving the kitchen. 'It's so good to have you back where you belong, Jan,' she said softly. 'Kyle's the happy man he used to be, with the added bonus of being a father now. I mention that because—well, you seem a little sad sometimes, Jan. You *are* happy to be back, aren't you?'

'This is where my life is,' Jan said simply, and Deirdre flashed a relieved smile.

'Then everything's fine,' she said, beaming her satisfaction as she went from the kitchen.

Jan busied herself with the large coffee urn designed for the number of people they were entertaining tonight, but her hands worked independently from her mind.

'Not quite fine,' she murmured aloud, 'but after tonight it will be. It has to be.' Kyle would inevitably show at least some displeasure at not having been told the truth, at having been cheated of his son's baby-hood, but when she explained ...

The remainder of the evening flew by on winged seconds, the last hour of the party being spent in several of the younger couples dancing to stereo music in a cleared space near the front door where the light was dimmer. Kyle danced dutifully with some of the other women, but had Jan in his arms most of the time. The music he had chosen to play had a slow and sensuous beat to it, and she felt the tension in his body, the warmth of his breath against the black fall of silky hair beside her cheek.

'How long do we have to wait before throwing them all out?' he half groaned into her ear, sending delicious shivers of anticipation through her. The swooning sensation in her knees made her pull away slightly and look up into the softened lines of his face.

'You haven't danced with Elena,' she reminded him huskily.

A frown settled like a thundercloud between his brows. 'Is there any rule that says I have to?'

'No ... of course not. It's just that she—you said she'd been helpful to you ... it doesn't seem right to ignore her now.'

His mouth tightened. 'If you'd been treated to the shrewish display she put on for me earlier you wouldn't be so soft-hearted about her either.' His hand grew firm on her spine. 'There was never anything between us, Jan. I didn't ask her to come over here and see to the renovations when I couldn't be here myself—it was just something she said she wanted to do. Oh, I tried kissing her a couple of times, more as an experiment than anything, but it didn't work. You know why, don't you?' His lips nuzzled her cheek, then came to claim her mouth in a sweetly lingering kiss.

'Anyway,' he said unsteadily, 'it seems Elena's taken the advice I gave her earlier. Stu's been in love with her for years, even though he married somebody else on the rebound.' His eyes turned to where Stu and

Elena danced nearby. 'They should have married years ago.'

But Elena was in love with you years ago, Jan wanted to say, but let the subject drop when Kyle pulled her closer, his body warm and taut against hers, Elena dismissed from his mind.

Then at last the goodbyes were being said, coats and boots being donned in deference to the crisp coldness of the starlit night. Shouted thanks and invitations for Jan and Kyle to pay return visits echoed back to them as the last guest tramped away on the cleared path through banked snow at either side.

Kyle pulled Jan into the house and closed the thick door, leaning against it with a sigh and reaching for her.

'That was the longest evening in memory,' he breathed at her ear, his lips tracing the soft outline of her cheek and jaw until they possessed her mouth and moved with slow passion there. 'I hope you're not going to suggest clearing up the mess tonight,' he muttered against her lips.

'Just—just a couple of things,' she whispered, finding pulling herself away from him almost too difficult. 'You go on up, I won't be long.'

'See that you're not.' The soft note in his voice held a hint of threat, but he made no move to stop her as she went to collect glasses on a tray to carry into the kitchen with her.

Most of the supper dishes had been done with the help of many additional hands, so there was no real need to worry about the final clearing up tonight, but Jan felt an overwhelming need to be completely alone for a few minutes. She had to plan in her mind and heart how best to tell Kyle the news he wanted to hear, yet she knew he would be understandably upset, even annoyed, at having been kept in the dark for so long.

Words formed and disappeared as she moved about the kitchen, switching off the heat under the coffee, and finally turning off lights on her way upstairs. The right words would come, she decided in the upper hall, more sincerely for being unrehearsed. .

The uncanny silence in the master bedroom prompted her to call out uncertainly: 'Kyle?', but there was no answer, just an eerie kind of stillness, a quiet that seemed to wait ...

'Ky——'

His name broke off sharply on her lips as she came to the open door separating Robbie's room from hers. Kyle stood at the end of the crib, a hand on each side of the gaily painted bars supporting him as he bent over the foot of the bed.

Jan's eyes flew in the same direction his took and a hand seemed to squeeze the blood from her heart. Robbie had kicked off the sheets and blankets in his tossing, baring the feet she had not covered with sleepers that night because he had worn socks and slippers for downstairs.

'Kyle!' she breathed, stricken as his head and shoulders lifted as if in slow motion and eyes deadened with shock in a grey-tinged face focused on her. His voice held the same greyness.

'He's mine, isn't he? Robbie's my son!'

CHAPTER ELEVEN

Robbie's quick, light breathing was all that broke the tension-wrought silence between them. Jan nodded mutely, unable to take her eyes from the tortured anguish in Kyle's, and equally unable to force words through her closed throat.

'Why, Jan, why?' The question came in a voice oddly broken and edged with disbelief. Then as she watched, she saw the bemused outline of his face tauten whitely to anger. He strode to her and gripped her flaccid wrists in a bonecrushing grasp.

'You—you *bitch*! Why did you let me think Paul was his father? That I couldn't—oh *God*, don't you know what you did to me?'

He shook her violently while his voice seared her, her hair bouncing and floating away from her bared shoulders. The pain in her wrists numbed her, but tears rose to fill the darkened blue of her eyes.

'I—I was going to tell you,' she gasped. 'Tonight . . .'

'When?' he demanded harshly. 'While I was making love to you in bed? When I couldn't get angry with you for putting me through hell?' He threw her hands from him with a disgusted gesture. 'And why tonight anyway? Why couldn't it have been when you first came back?—or better still when you knew you were pregnant? Didn't you think I had a right to know you were carrying my child?'

She gazed helplessly at the drawn fury evident in every line of his body, every savage clench of his jaw and mouth.

'I—you—hated me. I was—afraid you'd take Robbie away from me.'

His breath rushed audibly through white flared

nostrils. 'In that at least you were right! You can stake
your life on my son staying here where he belongs!
Even if it means I have to take you back to keep him
here.' He flung away from her and slammed the outer
bedroom door behind him.

Jan stared sightlessly into space for several minutes,
the tears frozen on her cheeks. Everything had gone
wrong. Kyle hated her more than ever now, and meant
what he said about keeping Robbie with him, with or,
preferably, without her. He hadn't been showing love
when he made love to her; he had calculated that that
was the surest way of keeping her, and thus Robbie, at
Silvercreek. But now that he knew Robbie was his son,
there would be no need to shroud how he really felt
about her.

Robbie stirred and murmured in his sleep and she
walked stiffly, automatically, to his side, covering up
the exposed telltale limbs. As she stroked the soft dark
hair from his forehead she knew that she would never
give him up voluntarily.

Wasn't that what this had all been about?—the
secrecy, the deception? Robbie was hers far more
deeply than he could ever be Kyle's ... it was her
breast his baby mouth had sought, her hands that had
cared for him, her voice that had sung him to sleep
countless times. Kyle knew nothing of all that.

There would be other women for him, and a special
one who would give him the son he wanted now that
he knew he could father a child ... a woman he could
live at peace with ...

Dawn was already streaking pink scrolls across the sky
when Jan at last fell into sleep, a drugged sleep only
vaguely disturbed by the sound of male voices coming
from a distance. The sound meant nothing to her,
however, and she had forgotten it until she went with
Robbie to the kitchen shortly after nine and found a
note, as cryptic as the one Kyle had left her on her first
morning.

'Have to go to emergency at Green Meadows.' Here the period sign had been heavily overlaid, as if Kyle had had to think before carrying on with the hasty scrawl. 'We have to talk, but that will have to wait till I get back. Before dark, I hope.' There was a heavy dash and a starkly outlined 'K'—no softness, no gentleness, in the writing as forceful as Kyle himself, and Jan bit her lip as she put on coffee for herself and eggs scrambled in milk for Robbie.

Unwittingly, Kyle had given her the chance of escape. The Green Meadows cabin, part of the Masters empire, lay in a direction paralleling the main highway into town. If she took the other direction ... She frowned thoughtfully and leaned against the counter looking out across the lake and distant mountains shrouded in grey.

The other direction led to the lumber camp, which in turn led to the main highway to Williams Lake. If she could get that far, a plane would take her and Robbie to the anonymity of Vancouver ... should she ask Don for help yet again? No, she decided, lifting a cup from the cupboard and pouring the first of the comfortingly hot brew to sip it with eager lips. Don had helped her before because he thought there might be a chance of her loving him in return one day. Now there was no hope of that, ever. No matter how much Kyle hated her, and would go on hating her, there could be no other man in her life.

She blinked and directed her thoughts away from that dangerous—and futile—subject.

There was still the problem of transport. Even if a motor vehicle could reach the lumber camp, it was likely that Kyle and the other men had taken every available mobile transport to the easily accessible Green Meadows. It was Robbie who gave her the idea of using the time-honoured mode of conveyance in the Cariboo.

'Ride with Gypsy, Mommy?' he wheedled as she laid the scrambled eggs before him.

'Yes, darling,' she returned thoughtfully. 'We'll ride with Gypsy today.'

Harnessing Gypsy to the sleigh would pose no problem, she had done it several times when Kyle was unavailable. The mare's gentle plodding would bring them into reach of the lumber camp long before Kyle arrived home ... she could think of an excuse on the way for enlisting the aid of the lumber men in reaching Williams Lake. Gypsy could be returned later to the ranch.

Busying herself in the kitchen clearing away all vestiges of the previous night's party, then tidying the living areas in the house kept her misgivings at bay. It gave her a forlorn kind of satisfaction to look round the spruced-up rooms and know that at least Kyle wouldn't come home to a mess. An empty house, but no mess.

She packed a minimum of essentials in a soft grip bag, knowing Robbie was too young to observe or care as long as Gypsy pulled him in state across the snow-covered meadows.

It was well after midday before they were on their way, Robbie looking forward expectantly as the gentle Gypsy traversed territory new to him at Jan's direction. Trees frosted and bent with the weight of recent snow grew thicker around them as the sleigh's runners swished across the virgin whiteness to where Jan estimated the lumber camp to be. The sun was her guide, a pale globe glinting off snowy rills and making them sparkle with diamond hardness. Gypsy's breath hung and froze in the clear air as she stamped doggedly on, head bent and responding automatically to Jan's gentle reminders on the reins.

Robbie's excited chatter died away as new country opened up in front of them. 'Robbie tired. Go home now, Mommy?' he asked hopefully.

'Sleep on Mommy's lap, darling,' she said, and gathered him up into her arms, one round him and the other guiding the reins. 'We'll soon be there.'

'Soon be home,' he agreed contentedly, and promptly fell asleep on her shoulder.

The sun was obscured suddenly as they entered a denser belt of trees, firs whose wrinkled bark seemed to squeak in protest against the cold air disturbed in the sleigh's passage through them. Gypsy automatically followed the rough trail, barely wide enough to take the ranch pick-up truck, which Kyle had cut through the forest. Jan's heart lightened a little as she glanced at her watch. The lumber camp must lie in this direction, and with any luck she and Robbie could be well on their way to Vancouver before dark. If there was a plane, and if there were vacant seats on that plane.

Luck had been with them so far, Jan thought, settling further down into the seat and hearing in her imagination the distant sound of saws biting into the hard creamy sap, the ring of men's voices on the crisp air.

Half asleep herself, Jan suddenly jerked into wakefulness, her arm tightening round the sleeping child. Something had happened ... the sleigh had stopped moving. Gypsy, ears at the alert, was staring into the thick growth to one side of the trail.

A noise came, one Jan vaguely remembered from her dreamlike state of a moment before ... the snap of dry, dead wood under a foot ... man's or beast's? Gypsy gave a frightened whinny and decided not to wait and find out. She took off along the trail at a speed she had not known for years, the sleigh careening wildly behind her, but it wasn't until the runners hit a half-hidden tree stump and dumped the two humans into the deep snow bordering the trail that Robbie woke with a piercing yell that resounded through the woods.

Dazed, Jan watched the horse and sleigh vanish round the next bend and her: 'Hush, darling, it's all right,' was completely automatic.

How far were they from the lumber camp and help?

More important, how dangerous was the unknown object which had frightened Gypsy into stampeding panic? Half-remembered tales of winter-hungry wolves and coyotes brought sickening dryness to her mouth, and her fearful eyes sought for danger in the closely spaced trees while she sat winded beside the trail, rocking the sobbing child instinctively. Another tentative snap came from the gloomy interior, then a slight pause before a crashing sound, indicative of a hasty retreat, reached her ears.

'It's all right, darling,' she repeated, cradling Robbie to her heart as relief flooded through her. If only they could reach the camp before the creature, whatever it was, returned to investigate further.

Jan struggled to her feet and struck off along the trail, her boots squeaking as they dug into snow half flattened by the sleigh's runners in Gypsy's precipitate retreat. Where would the horse go? Perhaps she was already at the camp and help was on its way. If the bag with their possessions in it was still wedged into the sleigh, the men would know there had been an accident and investigate.

Robbie's sobs quietened as she trudged along, but Jan's breath was soon coming in deep pants because of his weight and the awkwardness of carrying him in the bulky snow suit. She was almost delirious with relief when, minutes later, they emerged from the darkness of trees to sloping meadowland, and she saw the cluster of prefabricated buildings in the distance.

'We're almost there now,' she gasped her relief to Robbie who looked up to her face, hope shining in his dark eyes.

'Daddy there?'

'Lots of daddies,' she assured him shortly, ignoring his wide-eyed look of astonishment.

She trudged across the snow, mind and eyes fixed on the safety awaiting them in the huddled buildings, then halted suddenly and narrowed her eyes, her breath puffing quick clouds of vapour into the air.

Something was wrong. No sign of life came from the buildings, no wisp of smoke rising to the blue sky above, no whining saw indicating that the men were busy on a far slope. Instead there was an air of desolation, abandonment about the camp.

Closer investigation revealed that the small settlement was indeed deserted. Only the tracks of unknown animals marked the most recent fall of snow, and Jan's heart plummeted in despair. How far along the roughly slashed lumber road did the main highway to Williams Lake lie? Five miles?—ten? It could possibly be only two, but a glance at the lowering sun told her there was no possibility of finding out that day before darkness covered the open hillsides and forests.

There was nothing else for it but to spend the night here at the camp and start early in the morning. Unless ...

Her steps slowed and stopped as her eyes sought and found the machine shed where equipment must be kept. Wasn't it possible that a vehicle of some kind had been left by the departed loggers? A quick inspection of the big double doors convinced her of the hopelessness of breaking the heavy padlocks securing them ... of course the men would have seen to the protection of the expensive equipment inside.

The cookhouse was similarly barred against the entry of strangers, and Jan was half sobbing with fright and frustration when she carried Robbie, growing heavier with each step, to a cabin set apart from the main buildings.

The door opened to her touch and her eyes filled with tears of relief as she stepped inside the plain but neatly kept one-room cabin. Dimly, she remembered Kyle telling her that in some isolated spots, following long tradition, unused cabins would be left open for the use of travellers caught short by the sometimes harsh climate. 'It can be a matter of life and death,' he had told her seriously, 'and very few people abuse the courtesy.'

Now Jan sent up a prayer of thankfulness to the hardy pioneers who had initiated that tradition. Robbie, if not both of them, could have perished in the bonechilling cold of the Cariboo night.

She set Robbie down from her aching arms and looked round. She almost expected the laid kindling and stack of small-cut logs beside the black Franklin stove, the cupboard above a makeshift sink to hold varied sized cans of food supplies. Rough grey blankets were folded neatly on the room's single bunk, which indicated that the occupant was probably the logging foreman when operations were under way.

'Robbie hungry, Mommy!'. The childish pipe, frankly complaining, brought her mind back to more practical considerations. First, the fire.

Blessing the one who had laid it ready, even to supplying a box of thick wooden matches, Jan set a light to the paper and kindling and in moments the dry wood was ready for the application of heavier pieces. In what seemed no time at all, the small room was filled with scented warmth from the pine logs and Jan unzipped Robbie's snow suit after dealing with her own jacket. She settled him on a worn settee close to the fire while she made a closer inspection of the supplies.

A feeling of excitement gripped her, a sense of oneness with those pioneers of old who had braved this unknown land with all its hardships ... though her own plight was far removed from the stringent conditions they had faced. Canned potatoes, baked beans, various meats and vegetables were all there in reasonable abundance. There was even coffee in a vacuum pack, and she unearthed a battered metal pot from another cupboard which held pots and dishes.

There was no running water, but a scoop of fresh snow from near the cabin melted quickly on the broad stove top, and soon the aroma of fresh coffee mingled with the scent of pine in the small room. While it brewed, Jan busied herself with the opening of cans of corned beef, new potatoes and baby carrots, placing the vegetables to warm beside the coffee pot.

Robbie, thawed out and feeling lively, bounced on the aged sofa springs and watched her prepare their meal, tucking into it hungrily fifteen minutes later when they sat side by side at a worn wooden table under the small window. The limited span of his consciousness accepted this new adventure without question. Jan, the centre of his world, was there, her smiles and occasional gurgling laughs warm and familiar. He was quite oblivious of the effort those smiles and laughs cost her.

'Daddy come soon?' he asked guilclessly when the meal was over.

Jan hesitated, then took what she told herself was the coward's way out. 'Not tonight, sweetheart.'

'Daddy come in the morning,' he stated confidently, and slid down from the chair unworriedly. Even being put to bed by the light of candles some time after darkness had filled the small square of window held little strangeness for him, his mother sitting beside him telling the stories and singing the songs long familiar to him.

But when at last he slept, the flush on his checks tonight only that beamed from the fire's warmth, Jan sat alone on the old sofa, staring at the leaping flames in the freshly stoked stove, her thoughts pensive.

Long before now Kyle would have returned to the ranch and discovered their disappearance. What, if anything, would he do? There was little he could do in the way of pursuit, even if Gypsy had returned dragging the empty sleigh. Tracks would be obscured by darkness, and by the time daylight made them visible Jan would be starting off on the logging trail to the highway.

She sighed, pulling the single blanket she had taken from the bed closer round her though it was needed only for the security it provided; the room was warm, almost too warm from the glowing stove ... Away in the distance, like a disembodied voice, an animal howled, desolate with longing. A wolf? ... coyote? ... Jan slept.

Shadows flitted noiselessly across her muted consciousness ... grey shapes coming on padded feet towards the cabin from behind the machinery shed ... dogged intentness in the thrust of pointed heads ... bared red tongues and glinting white teeth ...

Terror closed her throat to the wild screams gathered in her chest as the animals drew nearer, their paws now seeming to be clothed in boots ... boots that scrunched and squeaked across the snow. And then the massive bodies were throwing themselves against the door, pounding, rattling the handle ...

Now Jan uttered a strangled scream and started up, terrified eyes reaching fearfully for the door and seeing it open, a dark figure obscuring the brightness of moonlight outside the cabin.

'Jan? What is it, Jan?'

Kyle's gruff man's voice sent a weakening flood of relief through her as the nightmare faded. The candles flickered in the cold gust of air as Kyle turned to close the door, throwing off the hood of his parka before coming quickly to bend over her.

'Jan, are you okay? Did something frighten you?'

'Ju—just a dream.' She looked wonderingly round the small room, at the fire reduced to a dull red glow, the candles flickering on the table, and lastly sitting up to look over the back of the sofa at Robbie, miraculously still sleeping in peace.

'Is he all right?' Kyle's eyes, bright and hard, went to the bunk where Robbie's dark head was visible above the blankets.

'Yes, he ... we found things to eat. I lit the fire,' she said dazedly.

'Thank God you did,' he said fervently. 'You'd have died out there if you'd wandered around.'

Of themselves the words denoted concern, yet there

was a curious lack of expression in the clear-cut outline of Kyle's face. Strain had deepened the lines round
eyes and mouth, and tiredness made his broad shoulders seem less confident as he went to re-stock the stove
after shrugging off his thick jacket. Even before he
turned back to her, flames were shooting up round the
dried wood, making it crackle and cascade sparks
through the wide bars.

Then he was sitting beside her, one thigh firm and
vibrant against her side, his fingers fastening round
her chin with chilly force to raise her eyes to the hot
fury raging in his.

'Don't *ever* do that to me again!' The controlled
anger in his voice cracked on the last word, and suddenly she was pulled roughly into his arms, feeling the
violent trembling of his body, hearing the muffled,
broken words against her incredulous ear. 'Oh, Jan ...
darling ... went crazy ... find you, couldn't ...'

Everything seemed crazy to her all at once. Won-
derfully, marvellously crazy, but ...

'How did you know where we were?' she faltered,
too conscious of his unshaven chin against her cheek.
'It's dark.'

His eyes held a suspicious glint of moisture when he
raised his head to look into hers.

'It's as bright as day outside, darling. Gypsy came
home with the empty sleigh, except for the bag you
had packed, and I knew you couldn't be too far away.'
His eyes and voice reflected deep-seated agony. 'Jan,
why did you go? Didn't you see my note?'

'I saw it.' She turned her head away. 'You wanted to
talk, to take Robbie away ... you didn't want me, and
I—I couldn't leave him.'

The logs in the stove suddenly caved in on themselves, the only sound to break the silence between
them. Then Kyle said intently:

'Jan, look at me.' His fingers forced her chin up
until her eyes glanced off the intense brown of his. 'I

wanted Robbie, yes,' he said with slow deliberation, 'but only because he's part of you, and part of me ... the living symbol, if you like, of what we once had together.'

'But—but you said, last night——'

'I know what I said last night,' he interrupted grimly. 'I fouled up again, after telling myself I never would if I had a second chance.' Ignoring her startled gasp, he went on: 'I did a lot of thinking last night, Jan, after I left you. A lot of it was centred on the unbelievable fact that Robbie was my son, not Paul's. But something else kept tapping at the back of my mind, something I couldn't remember until it was almost dawn.'

'You stayed up all night?' she asked, startled.

He gave her a tight smile. 'It was very important to me that I remember. Anyway, I finally recalled what you said that night I suggested we make a home together for Robbie—do you remember? You said it wouldn't work because you'd never love anyone but his father. I thought then you were talking about Paul, that he was the dead love you spoke about.' The tenor of his voice dropped to pained huskiness as his hand came up to stroke the silky darkness of her hair from her forehead. 'It never died for me either, Jan.'

Contradictory thoughts ripped through Jan's mind and heart as she stared up at him. Tension coiled like a spring in her stomach and she sat up straight with a sudden movement.

'Kyle, I—I'm all mixed up. Will you—could you—make some coffee or something?' She needed time to think, time to adjust to the new emotions raging chaotically through her.

Hesitation was only momentary, then Kyle nodded and got to his feet, seeming glad to have something practical to do in the primitive cabin which crackled with emotive tension. He went outside for snow to melt for coffee, as she had earlier, and when he finally brought the steaming mug of rich black liquid to the sofa, Jan had gathered a measure of composure round her.

They sipped in silence for several minutes, each occupied with their own thoughts until Jan said with remarkable calmness: 'You say that our—love—had never died for you. But when I came back you—hated me.'

'I've never hated you, Jan,' he denied hoarsely. 'Except for that one night when I thought you and Paul— oh God, I could have killed both of you that night.' Blindly he put down his coffee on the floor and buried his face in his hands, his voice quelled by the agony shaking him. 'Paul was always attractive to women, he had that kind of personality. I never minded the casual girl-friends he took from me, none of them meant very much ... I just didn't think he could take you from me.'

His hands came down from his face, but he didn't look at Jan, who felt the sudden erratic pounding of her heart. Now, three years later, she was hearing for the first time how Kyle had felt that night.

'Gran heard me come home and called me into her room. She said I should know what had been going on while I was away, that you and Paul—had been laughing and carrying on a love affair in the living room.'

'We laughed, yes,' Jan said coldly, remembrance sending a chill through her bones. 'Paul was good company, and I was glad of that while you were away. But did you really think we'd "carry on", as she put it, in the next room to hers? If that had been what we wanted, there were lots of places much more private we could have picked!'

Kyle ran a hand over his chin, rasping the blue-black growth of stubble. 'I told her that, and a few other things. Nevertheless, I guess I was prepared for what I saw when I went into our bedroom.'

'What you thought you saw,' Jan corrected bitterly.

'Paul hadn't laid a hand on me until that night, and then it was only because he heard you come back earlier than expected and thought it would be hilarious for you to think ... what you did think. Oh, Kyle,' she cried, 'how could you have believed what you did? You knew the kind of sick humour Paul had at times.'

'Yes, I knew,' he agreed soberly. 'It took me only a day or two to remember that, then I——' he broke off and looked levelly into her eyes. 'I went to Vancouver, humble and ready to apologise. Paul's was the only address I knew there, and I guessed he'd know where I could find you. So I went to his apartment building ... sat in the car for a while, trying to get up the courage to go in. Then I saw you and Paul come out together and knew that you were staying there with him——'

'You knew no such thing!' she cried indignantly, lowering her voice when Robbie stirred restlessly behind them. 'You jumped to conclusions again, Kyle. Yes, I stayed at Paul's apartment, but he wasn't there. He lived with his sister two blocks away! He offered me his apartment while he was away on the engineering job, but I refused. I was only there for a few weeks until I found a cheaper place to live, where I could be in—independent.' Tears ran from her eyes and distorted her voice. 'He wanted to c-call you and explain again, b-but I wouldn't let him. If you d-didn't love me enough to—to *believe* that I could n-never ...' Gasping sobs overruled her voice then, but Kyle made no move to comfort her. Instead he sat as if carved from stone, elbows on knees, a hand pressed to each temple.

When at last he did look at her, his face reflected such misery that she wasn't sure if the blur of tears was in her eyes or his. His voice came out as little more than a hoarse whisper.

'I'm sorry, Jan—you'll never know how sorry. I lived in misery, in hell, for eighteen months after you left. Then Gran died, but before she did she told me she'd been wrong about you, that she'd lied because ...'

'Because she thought you'd divorce me and marry Elena, the one she'd always wanted for you,' Jan filled in dully.

He nodded soberly. 'But don't blame her too much for that, Jan. She couldn't see anyone as beautiful as you, as inexperienced in our ways of life, settling here on a permanent basis. We've lost quite a few good men because the women they married couldn't take it. She thought she was doing the best thing for me.'

'She didn't even give me a chance, Kyle,' Jan pointed out quietly.

'I know, honey, I know she didn't, and I regret that too.' He heaved a weary sigh. 'So did she, towards the end.'

'Kyle, you're tired,' she said, sudden tenderness touching her voice. 'No sleep last night, and tonight —what time is it, anyway?'

He glanced at the watch on his wrist. 'Just after eleven. I came in the truck—it wouldn't take us too long to get home.'

'No,' she decided, stirring and swinging her feet to the floor. 'It's more important that you have some sleep first. I can bunk down with Robbie if you can manage on the sofa.'

His strong hands reached for her waist and pulled her between his knees. 'I'd like it a lot better if you'd bunk with me instead of Robbie,' he said unsteadily.

Jan shook her head and pushed against his shoulders to free herself. 'No, Kyle, you need rest more than anything else right now. Besides, I—I'm pretty mixed up in my head at this moment. I have to think.' She drew a shuddering breath. 'It will be a lot more comfortable for you if you take off your boots,' she said with an unsuccessful attempt at lightness. She turned swiftly away. 'I'll put some more wood on the stove.'

When she turned away from the replenished grate, Kyle had taken off his heavy laced boots and was lying back on the creaking sofa, his head against the scarred plush at one end, his feet extended well over the other.

His hand caught her wrist and pulled her down to sit beside him, his fingers gentling but keeping their hold.

'You'll come home with me, Jan? You and Robbie?'

Her lower lip trembled in the same way as Robbie's when he was on the verge of tears. 'If—if you really want me.'

His hand lifted to her nape, dislodging the pins from her hair so that it fell suddenly as a curtain at each side of her face. Drawing her down until she was inches from his mouth, so close that she could feel the warmth of his breath against her skin, he said with savage quietness:

'*Want* you? I love you, Jan ... there's never been anyone else for me. I've never stopped loving you.'

It took a superhuman effort for Jan to push away from the confining hold of his fingers, but she did it, putting a safer distance between them.

'Yet you—hated me when I—came back.'

'I didn't hate you,' he gritted. 'I just couldn't think of any other way to get you to come and then to stay.' His breath was expelled in a gusty sigh. 'After Gran died, and I realised I'd been the one to throw you and Paul together whether you wanted it or not, I couldn't think of anything but getting you back—even if it meant tearing you away from Paul. I made enquiries and found out that he'd given up the Vancouver apartment not long after you and he left here ... I thought you must have gone with him on the engineering job, that that was the reason you hadn't asked me for a divorce. Then I saw you on that documentary film, just for a minute, but I knew then that at least you weren't with Paul.'

'So why didn't you come to me then?'

His other hand ran a crooked path through his hair, leaving a boyish strand marking his brow. 'What could I offer that would entice you back here? I needed a reason for you to come, and a way of showing you that nothing had changed as far as I was concerned. It took almost another eighteen months to alter the house the way we had planned it together. I knew that if that didn't convince you, nothing would.'

'But you were so cold,' she whispered, 'so—hateful when I did come.'

The line of his jaw tautened. 'It wasn't as I'd imagined it. You came with a contingent of men, especially Don McLeish—you talked about marrying him. I blackmailed you into staying because I thought ... well, that with time I could win you back. I even arranged it so that we would be more or less alone at the ranch, that what we'd once had would flower again, I guess. I hadn't reckoned on Robbie then,' he continued wryly, 'or on being convinced that you were still in love with his father—Paul, as I thought.'

Jan closed her eyes against the well of feeling spurting inside her, making no resistance when Kyle drew her down to him again and found her lips with sudden hunger, moulding his own to them in a way that was possessive yet faintly questioning. His hands lifted her until she lay full length against the throbbing hardness of his body, her mouth capitulating to the insistent thrust of his.

He had talked of home, but she knew in that moment that home to her would always be where he was, in his arms, giving and receiving the love neither of them had been able to deny.

Slowly, reluctantly, he pulled slightly away from her lips. '*Are* you still in love with his father?' he probed huskily, his eyes pinpoints of wickedness.

'Do you have to ask?'

Her answer, breathed in the faintest whisper, seemed to satisfy him. A smile flitted across his mouth just before it reached for hers again. A smile of triumphant possession, yes ... but there was infinite tenderness there too, and a heartfelt thankfulness ...

'Set one camera up over here, will you, Hank?'

Don McLeish, the role of film-maker sitting comfortably on his capable shoulders, directed Hank Linden to a spot near the front door of Silvercreek House. From that angle, they could zoom in for shots of the fireside area where ranch employees as well as the rancher and his family enjoyed a token Christmas gathering.

It had been Kyle's suggestion that a pre-Christmas filming would enable the film company, as well as the employees at Silvercreek, to enjoy Christmas Day in their own homes.

'We can have some people in for the evening,' he had told Jan, 'but I'd like us to celebrate Christmas this year with a family dinner ... you, me and Robbie.'

'And maybe next year there'll be you, me, Robbie, and——?' she had teased with dancing eyes, growing more serious when he pulled her close to the hard length of his body.

'You think there might be another Masters in the making?' he had demanded. 'One I'll see as a baby this time?'

'It's much too soon to tell yet,' Jan had laughed, adding: 'But it won't be your fault if there isn't.'

'It won't, will it?' he replied with a complacency reminiscent of Robbie's. 'Anyway, I'd like to put in my order now for a little girl with black hair and the blue of heaven in her eyes. One who knows that her daddy loves her almost as much as he loves her mother.'

'I really think your order might have been placed already,' Jan had conceded, her voice betraying the upswell of love she would always feel for this man, and only him.

'I wonder how Robbie will take to competition,' he had mused, eyes going thoughtfully to where their son played happily nearby with the puppy Kyle had brought in from the barn a week before. 'He won't like your attention being diverted to a squalling brat.'

'What? My babies are never squalling brats,' she had protested indignantly, thereby revealing her hope that another child lay under her heart even then.

'I really don't care whether it squalls or not,' Kyle

had murmured huskily, 'as long as it's ours.'

Now as they took their places at the providentially long table, the newly returned ranch employees and their wives ranged on either side between Kyle and Jan, she reflected that on her part it was more of a thanksgiving dinner than the one celebrating the birth of a Babe long ago.

Thankfulness was hers in the juicy golden turkey she had cooked, the colourful vegetables and dressings laid at intervals along the sturdy table, but most of all in the invisible tie that brought her eyes to meet the glowing brown of her husband's. Love, strong and enduring, bathed them and all who sat at their table ... love that would suffice in all the years to come.

Strangely, it was Don who brought it all together for her.

'I don't think I've ever filmed a more perfect setting than this,' he said when at last the cameras had stopped whirring and he stood apart from the others with Jan. Her sensitive inner ear knew that his words conveyed much more than their surface intent.

'Yes ... it's perfect, isn't it?'

Do you have a favorite
Harlequin author?
Then here is an
opportunity you must
not miss!

3 GREAT NOVELS

Harlequin brings you a book to cherish ...

three stories of
love and romance
by one of your
favorite
Harlequin authors ...

What readers say about Harlequin Romances

"Your books are the best I have ever found."
P.B.*, Bellevue, Washington

"I enjoy them more and more
with each passing year."
J.L., Spurlockville, West Virginia

"No matter how full and happy life might be,
it is an enchantment to sit
and read your novels."
D.K., Willowdale, Ontario

"I firmly believe that Harlequin Romances
are perfect for anyone who wants to read
a good romance."
C.R., Akron, Ohio

*Names available on request